VENGEFUL VICE

BELLAMY BROTHERS FOUR

HELEN HARDT

HS
HARDT & SONS

This book is an original publication of Helen Hardt

Cover Design: Shepard Originals
Edited by Eric J. McConnell

Print ISBN: 978-1-952841-35-4

VENGEFUL VICE

BELLAMY BROTHERS FOUR

Helen Hardt

HELEN HARDT
WWW.HELENHARDT.COM

PRAISE FOR HELEN HARDT

"Literally perfection."

~**Read with Aimee** on *My Heart Still Beats*

"Helen Hardt is a master at making you fall for the bad boy."

~**Words We Love By** on *Savage Sin*

"Hardt spins erotic gold..."

~***Publishers Weekly*** on *Follow Me Darkly*

"22 Best Erotic Novels to Read"

~***Marie Claire* Magazine** on *Follow Me Darkly*

"Intensely erotic and wildly emotional..."

~***New York Times* bestselling author Lisa Renee Jones** on *Follow Me Darkly*

"Christian, Gideon, and now...Braden Black."

~**Books, Wine, and Besties** on *Follow Me Darkly*

"This red-hot tale will have readers fanning themselves."

~**Publishers Weekly** on *Blush*

"*Scintillating...*"

~**Publishers Weekly** on *Bloom*

"Helen's intelligent writing style and skills have made this story a must-read."

~**FireSerene Reads** on *Bloom*

"It's hot, it's intense, and the plot starts off thick and had me completely spellbound from page one."

~**The Sassy Nerd Blog** on *Rebel*

"This book was fantastic! It was steamy, funny, romantic, and just about any other emotion you can think of..."

~**Steamy Book Mama** on *Lily and the Duke*

"*Craving* is the jaw-dropping book you *need* to read!"

~***New York Times*** **bestselling author Lisa Renee Jones** on *Craving*

"Completely raw and addictive."

~**#1** ***New York Times*** **bestselling author Meredith Wild** on *Craving*

"Talon has hit my top five list...up there next to Jamie Fraser and Gideon Cross."

~***USA Today*** **bestselling author Angel Payne** on *Craving*

"Talon and Jade's instant chemistry heats up the pages..."

~**RT Book Reviews** on *Craving*

"Sorry Christian and Gideon, there's a new heartthrob for you to contend with. Meet Talon. Talon Steel."

~**Booktopia** on *Craving*

"Such a beautiful torment..."

~**Bare Naked Words** on *Craving*

"Made my heart stop in my chest. Helen has given us such a heartbreakingly beautiful series."

~**Tina, Bookalicious Babes** on the Steel Brothers Saga

"A dark, intoxicating tale."

~**Library Journal** on *Unchained*

"Helen Hardt has some kind of skill I don't have the words to describe. Her writing is addictive. She sucked in my mind and I just don't want to read anything but her right now!"

~**OMGReads Blog**

"Helen Hardt...is a master story teller."

~**Small Town Book Nerd**

In gratitude for all my good fortune.

PROLOGUE

VINNIE

The ballroom is buzzing with chatter, laughter, and the clinking of champagne glasses. Crystal chandeliers hang from the ceiling, casting sparkles over the elegantly dressed attendees. I stand near the entrance, greeting guests and keeping a watchful eye on the room. This event is crucial for the family's public image—and for my own plans.

I scan the crowd, pausing here and there on familiar faces. Politicians, businessmen, socialites—all here to support a good cause. The Raven's Wings Foundation is a noble effort, dedicated to funding blood cancer research and treatment. It's a legitimate cause, which makes my presence here all the more important.

Then I see her.

Raven Bellamy. The founder of the foundation, my sister's sister-in-law, and the woman who's captured my attention—my love—more than I can allow myself to admit. She's standing near the stage, talking to a small group of admirers. Her short dark hair, barely grown out after her battle with cancer, catches the light and frames her face in a way that's both striking and delicate.

She's beautiful. Not in the conventional, long-haired, magazine-cover way, but in a way that speaks of strength and resilience. Her dark eyes shine with a light that's hard to ignore, her smile genuine as she speaks to her supporters. There's something about her, something raw and real, that pulls me in.

Has pulled me in since the first time I laid eyes on her over a month ago, when her head was covered in dark peach fuzz. My heart beats faster in her presence, and my groin tightens. I can hardly breathe as images of devouring those full pink lips invade my mind. They were the softest and sweetest lips I've ever kissed.

I draw in a breath and walk toward her, the need to be close to her nearly overwhelming me.

I should stay away. I promised to stay away.

But damn...

I weave through the crowd and nod at people I mostly don't recognize. After all, I've only been back in this country a couple months. When I reach her, she's just finished her conversation and turns to face me.

"Vinnie," she says, her voice warm and inviting, as if what transpired between us never happened. "I'm glad you could make it."

"Raven." God, her lips. They glisten with a silvery effervescence. "I wouldn't miss it for the world. Congratulations on the event."

"Thank you," she says, her gaze locking onto mine. "It means a lot to have your support."

For a moment, we stand there, the noise of the ballroom

fading into the background. I'm struck by the depth in her eyes, the unspoken stories they hold. She's been through hell and back—part of it due to me—yet she stands here, a pillar of strength.

Does she remember what we shared?

What we said to each other?

Is her heart breaking like mine is in this moment—this moment when we must pretend to be mere acquaintances?

"I have to admit," I say, leaning in slightly, "I'm impressed by what you've accomplished. The foundation, your journey... It's inspiring."

Her smile widens, a faint blush coloring her cheeks. "That means a lot coming from you."

Does it?

Or is this part of the show?

Before I can respond, an amplified voice interrupts us.

"May I have your attention please."

I look toward the front of the ballroom where a man stands at the podium. Raven's father, Austin Bellamy, dressed like the Texas rancher he is. At first glance, his black tuxedo and crisp white shirt seem like normal cocktail attire, but the bolo tie with the turquoise gemstone slide shows his roots.

"Thank you all for coming this evening to our gala in support of my daughter's new foundation, Raven's Wings. We won't take up a lot of your time, but it's only proper that the founder herself say a few words. Come on up here, sweetheart."

Raven waves to me and makes her way through the crowd to step up to the microphone. The room falls silent, all eyes on her.

"Good evening, everyone," she begins, her voice clear and

strong. "Thank you all for being here tonight and for supporting the Raven's Wings Foundation for the research and treatment of blood cancers. This foundation is incredibly personal to me, and I'd like to share a bit of my story with you." She pauses and scans the room. "A few years ago, I was diagnosed with leukemia. It was the most terrifying moment of my life. The uncertainty, the pain, the endless treatments —it was a battle I wasn't sure I could win. At first, I was overwhelmed by fear and despair. The thought of losing my life, of leaving my loved ones behind, haunted me day and night."

The audience is silent, hanging on her every word.

"I remember the nights spent in the hospital, staring at the ceiling, wondering if I would ever see another sunrise. Each day was a struggle, not just physically but emotionally and mentally. The treatments were brutal. There were days I couldn't get out of bed, days I wanted to give up. But through it all, I found strength in the love and support of my family. They were my rock, my reason to keep fighting."

She takes a deep breath, her eyes glistening with emotion.

"My brother Falcon was my greatest support. When the doctors said the traditional treatments for my type of leukemia had failed and that I needed a bone marrow transplant, he was the only match out of three brothers and a twin sister. Without a second thought, he stepped up and gave me the ultimate gift."

Without a second thought? Raven's need got him an early release from prison, though I understand why Raven isn't mentioning that fact. Everyone here knows anyway.

"His bone marrow saved my life. His selfless act cured me, and I stand here today, cancer-free, because of him. Falcon, thank you from the bottom of my heart."

Across the room, I see Falcon Bellamy stand up and nod at his sister. He looks good in a tux, but it's so odd seeing him in anything other than ranch wear. My own sister, Savannah, is beaming next to him in a midnight-blue gown.

The audience applauds, some wiping away tears.

"But our journey didn't end there," she continues, her voice gaining strength. "Surviving cancer gave me a new purpose. I knew I had to give back, to help others facing the same battle. That's why I founded the Raven's Wings Foundation. Our mission is to fund research and provide treatment for blood cancers, to give hope to those who need it most."

She pauses, looking around the room, her gaze firm and determined.

"I want to share a moment that changed my perspective during my treatment. The night after the transplant, I should have been ecstatic, but I was feeling particularly low. I was tired of the pain, the uncertainty. I felt like I was losing myself. My brother Falcon sat beside me, held my hand, and told me that it was okay to be scared, that it was okay to feel weak. He reminded me that being strong doesn't mean never feeling fear or pain—it means pushing through despite those feelings. It was in that moment that I realized strength isn't about never falling. It's about getting back up every time you do."

I can almost hear the words in Falcon's voice. He was speaking about his time behind bars. According to Savannah—now Falcon's fiancée—he learned that survival on the inside depended on internal as well as external strength.

The room is silent. I look around at the awed faces. Everyone seems captivated by Raven's words.

"This foundation is not just about finding a cure. It's

about supporting patients and their families, about providing hope and strength to those in the darkest moments of their lives. Tonight, your generosity will help us continue this vital work. Together, we can make a difference. Together, we can give hope to those who need it most."

She steps back from the microphone and the room erupts in applause. As she makes her way down from the stage, she catches my eye and smiles.

As the applause dies down, I know two things for certain.

One—I've given up Raven Bellamy for her own good, but I'll never love another.

And two—

I will kill a man tonight to protect her.

1

RAVEN

A month earlier...*

Being healthy feels *awesome.*

Seriously awesome.

I sit on the back deck outside my parents' ranch house. It's early, but this is nothing new. I was born on a ranch, and ranchers get up before the sun. But I haven't been getting up before the sun since I got sick. I've slept a lot of my time away. Now that I'm cancer-free—so far at least—and my body is returning to normal, I love getting up early.

Was the sky always this blue?

I took so much for granted, like the color of the Texas sky. It's not simply blue. It's a brilliant blue—the kind of blue that makes you stop and stare. It's like I'm seeing it for the first time. The colors around me are more vivid, more intense. The green of the trees, the bursts of color from flowers—they all seem to pop in a way I never noticed before.

The air feels different too. It's fresh and crisp, filling my lungs with each deep breath I take. Another thing I used to take for granted—the simple act of breathing without effort, without pain. Now, every inhale is a gift, a reminder of how precious and fragile life truly is. A gentle and soothing breeze brushes against my skin, and I can't help but close my eyes and savor the sensation.

I think about how far I've come, how I've fought through the darkest days and nights. Those endless treatments, the uncertainty, the fear—they're behind me now. I've emerged on the other side, stronger and more appreciative of the little things. Like how the sun feels warmer, more comforting, as it bathes me in its golden light. Or how the sound of my brothers talking among themselves is reassuring rather than driving me insane because they're leaving me out once again.

Their voices are low, coming from inside the kitchen.

Do they know I'm out here?

I rise to say good morning when their words filter out to me. I drop my jaw.

"We've got to stop Dad," my brother Hawk says. "This can't happen."

"Yeah?" Falcon's voice. "Tell me how, and I'm on it. Fuck it all. After all these years..."

"Please fix this." The voice belongs to my youngest brother, Eagle, and his tone is anxious, full of fear. "I thought this was over. You promised me you'd fix it, Falcon."

"Jesus Christ, Eagle." This from Hawk again. "He already did time for a crime he didn't commit. What the fuck else do you want?"

"Easy," Falcon, my older brother says. "What's done is done. We can't change any of it. All we can do is make sure no one digs on that land. At least not until we can fix everything."

"And how the hell do you expect us to do that?" Hawk demands. "The excavation is Dad's call, not ours."

"I'm on it," Falcon says. "Don't worry. No one's going to be digging there anytime soon."

My heart is racing. What are they talking about? Falcon went to prison for—

I nearly jump out of my chair and run inside the kitchen.

All three of my brothers go silent.

"Yeah, I heard you," I say.

"What are you doing up, Raven?" Falcon asks. "You should be in bed. Resting."

"I've spent the last two *years* in bed, Fal." I cross my arms. "I'm done staying in bed. I got up early because I felt good. Fucking good. But now, I overhear my three brothers talking about—"

"Raven." Falcon's voice is stern. He's the only one of my brothers who's older than I am. But he's only a year older, and we're all adults here.

"Falcon," I say back to him. "Don't pull that *big brother* crap on me. You may have saved my life with your bone marrow, but—"

"Christ, Ray." He rubs his forehead. "I won't ever hold that over your head. I was happy to do it. I'm so glad I *could* do it. What we were talking about—it's…nothing."

"Not from what I heard," I say.

Eagle's eyes are bloodshot. My baby brother. I want to go to him, take him in my arms. Hold him and read him a story like I used to when we were kids.

Eagle is no longer a kid. He's twenty-five years old. But looking at him now—with Falcon and Hawk both glaring at him—I could swear he's still that wide-eyed little boy.

Falcon clears his throat. "Raven, what the three of us were talking about doesn't concern you. You have one thing to concentrate on right now and that's healing your body."

"Your bone marrow is doing a pretty good job of that for me," I say.

"Ray..."

I shake my head. "Don't try to protect me, Falcon. I'm getting my strength back day by day. It grows a little with each passing sunrise, along with my hair. So spit it out, all of you. What the hell is going on here?"

"Let it lie," Hawk says. "Please, Raven."

"Please," Falcon echoes.

I look into my older brother's dark eyes. He saw more than any young man should during his time in prison. He's become hardened. His eyes are more deep-set, the dimples on his cheeks now creases. He's only thirty—still a young man. But incarceration ages you, and my brother is no exception.

He's also my Achilles heel. His bone marrow saved my life.

If he's going to ask me to look the other way, I can do it. I can do it for the person who saved me.

"Please," Falcon says again. "I could never live with myself if something happened to you. If you didn't allow yourself the time to fully heal."

"I don't want to worry about you guys," I say.

Falcon nods. "You never have to worry about me, Ray. If there's one thing I know how to do, it's how to take care of myself."

"Do you?" I tilt my head.

He raises an eyebrow. "You think I got through prison on my good looks alone?"

Falcon can always make me smile. He's the one who sat at my bedside after the transplant when I was feeling so sick and weak. He told me how to be strong, how to face every adversity, even when fear was threatening to eat me alive. He's the one who taught me that courage isn't the lack of fear. It's facing your fear, because something else is far greater than the fear. Do I believe he can take care of himself? Of course I do.

"What about Hawk and Eagle?"

Eagle says nothing.

But Hawk is never one to keep quiet. He's the first person to call out any kind of injustice. He hates unfairness of any kind. "Everything's fine, Ray. Please trust us on that."

Hawk doesn't lie.

So I choose.

I choose to trust my brothers.

I choose to look the other way.

At least for now.

2

VINNIE

The weight of the world presses down on my shoulders as I sit in my grandfather's office in an Austin skyscraper. It's different from his study at his home, where the room is heavy with the scent of leather and old books and the walls are lined with the faces of my ancestors, their stern eyes watching me, judging me. I can almost hear their whispers, feel their expectations.

This office is sleek and modern. Polished glass walls overlook an expanse of cityscape, the hum of Austin's daily grind a white noise that filters through the silence. The floor is made of polished white marble, and a handful of abstract art deco paintings adorn the inner walls. The furniture is minimalist. A small table and chairs next to a small wet bar, and a mahogany desk crowning the room, the only nod toward tradition in an otherwise futuristic space. Across from the desk are two red plush wingback chairs.

I can't feel the judgmental gazes of my ancestors here. There are no prodding eyes carved into age-old oil portraits, no oppressive atmosphere of legacy. There are a handful of framed portraits of the family—though my father is noticeably absent from all of them—on the desk, but they face my grandfather, not me. The only face I see is the stoic one in front of me.

The face of the man I've come to know as evil incarnate.

This isn't the life I wanted. I escaped it for over a decade, lost a brother and nearly a sister in the process. Watched my father go to prison for murdering Miles McAllister, the son of a rival family here in Texas.

And now?

This is the life I've been handed.

The life I came back to.

Willingly.

I had my reasons.

Mario Bianchi sits behind his desk, his gaze stern as he glares at me. He's a hard man, ruthless and feared by many, including the McAllister family.

"I'm happy you've returned, Vincent," he says. "I know you'll make me proud of you."

Right. I know my grandfather better than to take his words at face value. I fled to Europe after he showed me his true colors the year I turned eighteen. For him to be proud of me? To trust me?

I'm going to have to prove myself.

And it won't be pretty.

I glance over my grandfather's head and out the window at the city of Austin sprawling below, alive with its own pulse. I used to dream of a different life, one far away from the shadow of this family business. I left the country to make it happen, but I learned only that I am what my family made me.

Those dreams seem like distant memories now, replaced by the stark reality of what I must do.

My mother and sister are everything to me. Savannah is engaged to Falcon Bellamy, the son of a billionaire Texas rancher. Falcon's an ex-con, and he's strong and resilient. I watched him stay alert after several of my grandfather's henchmen pummeled the shit out of him. Miles McAllister, who wanted—no, that's not the right word. Was being forced—to marry Savannah, had a gun pointed to Falcon's head when my father, Vincent Gallo Senior, shot Miles before he could take Falcon out.

But Falcon was ready to go. He'd do anything for Savannah. That's how I know she's protected.

My mother, on the other hand…

With Dad now incarcerated, she's *my* responsibility. And she's a mess. She blames Savannah for everything, but she'll see reason eventually. She's an intelligent woman.

I stand, showing Grandfather my full height. I'm several inches taller than he is and a lot more muscular. Plus he's in his eighties.

"I'm willing to do what needs to be done," I say, burning my gaze into his, "but let's stop beating around the bush. I know what you expect of me. And if you think you're going to shove anything up my ass like you did when I was a kid, think again. I'll do what has to be done, but I won't be abused."

Grandfather shakes his head with a chuckle. "You think I was abusing you? You think I did anything to you that wasn't done to me?"

"Then you're a victim as much as I am," I say. "I won't run this family that way. I won't abuse people into obedience.

People will do my bidding because they respect me. Not because I hurt them."

Grandfather narrows his eyes. "So if I tell you that you have to violate an up-and-coming young man in the family, you will refuse?"

"I will absolutely refuse, Grandfather." I grit my teeth. "You want me to be back. I'm back. The first son of your only child. I'm here to do my duty, but if you expect me to run this family when you're gone, I'm going to do it my way."

Grandfather scowls. "Don't be an idiot, Vincent. You think you can command respect without having your men fear you?"

"I don't have to fucking rape them to get them to fear me."

He slams his hands on his desk, scattering several documents to the floor. "Why don't you ask your brother-in-law, Falcon Bellamy, about how many prisoners he fucked while he was in the slammer?"

I draw a breath and count to ten. I know my brother-in-law. I know he didn't do anything like that. In fact, he protected his men from it. He ruled his cell block the same way I'll rule this family. Through strength. Perceived strength.

"Say what you want about Falcon," I say. "I know the truth."

"You don't think he got his rocks off with any of those pretty boys?" A small grin cracks under his stony stare. "Surely you're not that ignorant."

"I'm not ignorant," I say. "Let me tell you this, Grandfather. The next time you violate anyone—and I mean *anyone* —I'll fucking murder you in your sleep."

He laughs then—a deep guttural laugh. "Damn, Vinnie. You might just have what it takes after all."

He has no fucking idea. "Just get on with it. Tell me what I have to do to prove myself so you'll step down. Who do I have to off?"

He laughs again. "You think it's that simple?"

"Tell me, then." I slowly sink into one of the chairs across his desk. "I admit I've been away for a long time. Tell me what I have to do to gain your trust and take over. As long as it doesn't entail shoving anything up anyone's ass, I'll do it."

"What if I tell you to kill someone?'

This time I laugh. How naïve does he think I am? Of course he's going to tell me to kill someone. I expected that. All I need to know is who. A fucking name.

"Something funny?" he asks.

"*You* are. Who do you think you're talking to, old man? I may have been gone for over a decade, but I know how this shit works."

"Call it shit again, and I'll give it back to your father."

"You think he can run a family from prison?"

"He doesn't need to stay in prison. I can have him out by tomorrow if I want to."

I have no doubt that he's telling the truth. My father killed Miles McAllister to save Falcon for Savannah. I never knew the depth of love my father had for his children until I saw him do that. Too bad he couldn't have offed Mario here and saved Michael and me as well.

I hate thinking about Michael, or Mikey, as Sav and I used to call him. He was a kind and gentle soul, and I blame myself for his death. I was a kid of eighteen when I got the fuck out of here. I didn't think about my younger brother, didn't think about the fact that he was next in line.

Didn't think about what Grandfather would do to him. The same thing he did to me.

I fled.

And during all that time, there wasn't a minute that went by that my guilt didn't consume me.

"Don't insult my intelligence," I say. "You're just as glad to have my father in prison. He was a placeholder, and you and I both know it. I'm back now. I'm the true heir to this damned throne of yours, so tell me what I need to do. Quit beating around the bush. I want to get on with it."

"How much do you love your sister?" he asks.

"More than you'll ever know."

"You underestimate me, Vincent." He takes a deep breath in, tenting his fingers. "You think that because of what I do, I have no love for my family. That's simply not true."

"Raping me with a billy club was your way of showing love?" I scoff.

He doesn't react. "Yes, in my way."

"Bullshit." I get back on my feet. "You were exerting power over me. Showing me violence."

Grandfather shrugs. "That's what makes you strong."

"I disagree. Look at Mikey."

He frowns. "He was weak."

"He was what *you* made him. You forced him into a marriage he didn't want. Just like you're forcing me." I feel nausea curling up my throat, but I force it down. "My only consolation is that my intended is only eleven years old, so at least I don't have to marry her this second."

"True. You've got seven years to sow your wild oats, Vincent." He gazes out the window onto the bustling streets of Austin. "Unless you sowed them all out of the country."

"I sowed plenty," I say. "Once I'm married, I will be faithful to my wife."

Grandfather scoffs again. "No one is ever faithful to his wife."

"I'm sure you weren't."

"Of course I wasn't. Neither was your esteemed father."

He may be right. I don't know. My mother and father's marriage was arranged. He may well have been unfaithful to her. But one thing I do know. Despite the fact that he allowed Grandfather to violate me and probably Mikey, and despite the fact that he was going to force Savannah into marriage to Miles McAllister, he does love his children. All three of us. Of that I'm certain.

"I don't give a shit whether my father was faithful or not. Just tell me who I have to kill. Let's get it over with."

Grandfather nods. He gathers a few documents off his desk and stacks them neatly. "I've given this some thought," he says. "And I have unfinished business with your brother-in-law, Falcon Bellamy."

I shake my head. "Oh, no. I will not kill my sister's future husband. This isn't a damned movie and I'm not Michael Corleone."

"I want to see Savannah happy as much as you do. I know you don't believe this, but I love all of my grandchildren." He picks up a framed photo from the corner of his desk and studies it. "No one was sadder to see Michael die."

I resist rolling my eyes. "If not Falcon, then who?"

"Someone that will hurt him. One of his siblings, I think." He puts the photo down and strokes his chin. "Perhaps the one he just saved from her cancer. Raven Bellamy."

3

RAVEN

I need a project.

I have an idea of what I would like it to be. I would love my brothers' involvement, but they're clearly occupied with something else. Something they won't discuss with me.

So I decide to call my sister, Robin.

Robin and I are twins—fraternal, not identical—but we do look similar. Of course, it's easier to tell us apart now because she has gorgeous long dark hair.

And I don't.

Robin lives on the Bellamy land. She and I both have our own places, but I've been staying at the main house with Mom and Dad since I've been home for my recovery. I'm hoping it's only a few more days before I can move back to my own place.

Robin is a veterinarian, and she works here on the ranch. It's a weekday and she's no doubt busy, but I decide to call her anyway.

"Hey, sis," she says when she answers the phone.

"Hey, Robbie. I need your help."

"Sure. What do you need?"

"I need a project. I think I'd like to give back to the cancer community."

"Hold on a minute, Ray. You're still technically *part* of the cancer community. You need your rest. Falcon's bone marrow may have saved your life, but you're still in recovery. Have you forgotten that you left the hospital against medical advice?"

"It wasn't exactly against medical advice. They saw that the bone marrow was working, but they wanted me to stay there for observation. I was sick and tired of that fucking hospital bed, Robin. So I came home. And since I've been home, I've continued to thrive."

"Except for those few days when you contracted a virus and Mom and Dad had to run you back to the hospital."

"And it turned out to be only a virus. I'm fine. I'm healing." As I say this I realize my voice is raised. I take a deep breath and attempt to reel it back in. "I'm just so sick of hospitals."

"I understand that."

I can't help rolling my eyes. Robin says she understands. They all do. But in truth, none of them understand. They haven't lived it.

I won't say that to my sister though. She means well. Plus, I called to get her help.

"Don't worry. Mom is watching me like a hawk. And Falcon hardly leaves my side, despite the fact that he's newly engaged and should be at his own place with his fiancée. I'm fine. I need something to occupy my brain since Mom and Dad won't let me do any work around the ranch."

"All right. What did you have in mind?"

"I'd like to start a nonprofit organization. Something to benefit the research of blood cancers."

"Okay. That's a noble calling, Ray, but I can't help you with that. If it doesn't involve healing animals, I'm not your girl. I don't know anything about that kind of stuff."

"I don't either. We'll both be starting from scratch. I'll use my trust fund to set it up."

"Okay. I'll be happy to kick in as well. I think it's a great cause. But other than financially, I'm not sure how I can benefit you."

"I just need your support, Robin. I'm home with nothing else to do, so I can do the research. But I want to know you're behind me. You're my twin. I want you to be my partner in this."

Silence for a moment, until—

"I'm really touched, Ray. Truly."

"Who else would I ask?"

Robin doesn't answer. I can see why she's confused. She was always more like a brother than a sister to me. She matched the boys on everything they did around the ranch, while I was a little softer and gentler. Oh, I learned my way around the ranch. I can ride a horse with the best of them. But I'm happier at home, hanging out with Mom, learning to cook and make a home the way she does.

"I just want you involved, Robin. I'm hoping it'll bring us closer. One thing I learned when I was sick is that I don't ever want to take you or my brothers for granted again."

"You never did that."

But Robin is wrong. I lived my own life, separate from my sister and brothers. I chose a life different from what they chose. I was ready to leave the ranch behind. But no longer. Here is where I belong, and I want to get closer to my sister. After all, we shared the same space for nine months.

"Thanks for saying that," I tell my sister. "I appreciate it."

"I think you're being too hard on yourself, Raven."

Again, my sister means well, but she doesn't get it. When you survive cancer, you see the world differently. You appreciate every little thing, all the nuances. That includes the members of your own family. I appreciate them in a way that they probably don't appreciate me. Not to say that they aren't all thrilled that I'm still with them. I get that. I totally do. But they're not the ones who almost bit the big one. That's me. Now that I'm here and I have a high chance of living to a ripe old age, I want to spend time with my family. Truly get to know them. And as much as I love my brothers, I need to start with my twin sister.

"I'm not trying to be hard on myself," I say. "But I feel a need to do this. And I want you involved."

"I'll do whatever I can for you. You can have a big infusion from my trust fund to get you started. But I don't know that I can be of any other help. Work has been crazy lately, and—"

I hold back a sigh. Well, I tried. "No worries, Robin."

Another pause.

Finally, "You know what? Let's do it. What about the guys?"

Happiness surges into me. "They can certainly be involved if they want to."

I don't mention to Robin that they're keeping secrets from me. They're probably keeping them from her as well. And unlike me, she would go barreling into them and demand to know what's going on.

For their sake, I don't want that.

"Okay," she says. "Sounds great. Just let me know what you need."

"Thanks. I'm going to do some simple research on how to set up a nonprofit. That's the easy part. Our lawyers can do it quickly. Then I'll need to start figuring out how to fill our coffers, and then figure out who to give the money to."

"You could set up a grant," she says. "Organizations could apply for the money."

"Yeah, I'm sure we could do that. But honestly, I'd like for the money to go to actual people. People who need treatment but can't afford it. Or research facilities."

"Yeah. I bet Dad has an attorney who can help you with all of that."

"I agree. And I want you sitting on the Board of Directors with me."

She laughs lightly. "All right, Raven. I'd be honored."

"Thanks Robbie. Talk to you soon."

"Yeah. I'll be over this weekend to see you."

After I end the call, I find my mother.

"Mom, is Dad around?"

"Yeah, he's home today." She gestures down the hall. "He's in his office."

"Great." I walk through the large ranch house to the hallway that houses my father's office. I knock on the door.

"Who is it?"

"It's me, Daddy. Raven."

"Come on in, sweetheart."

I open the door. My father sits behind his desk, his eyes on his computer screen. He smiles when I walk in. Everyone smiles at me now. And I have to say I don't hate it.

"Daddy, I need your help."

"With what?"

"I need a project. I want to start a nonprofit organization to benefit the research and treatment of blood cancers."

Dad leans back in his chair. "That's a big undertaking, Raven."

"Yes, but I want to do it." I cross the study toward his desk and take a seat across from him. "I can't just sit around here doing nothing. I want to give back. I have a second lease on life, and I don't want to waste it. I realize I'm one of the lucky ones. If it weren't for Falcon's bone marrow—"

Dad holds up a hand. "Let's not go there, baby girl. It's over, thank God. You're going to live, and we need to just be grateful for that."

"I *am* grateful, Daddy. Falcon is sick and tired of me thanking him. But my point is that it *did* happen. And without Falcon... Well, we all know what would've happened. What about the people who weren't so lucky? What about the people who don't ever get a match? Or what about those who *do* find a match, but they die anyway? I want to help them all. I have the resources, and I want to do it. I just need you to point me in the right direction."

"I have no idea how to set up a nonprofit organization."

"I know you don't. But you have attorneys, Daddy."

"Land-use attorneys. Contract attorneys."

"You don't think any of them have a partner who might know what he's doing?"

Dad chuckles. "Of course. I'll find somebody for you, sweetheart." His face stiffens. "Are you sure you want to take this on? You're still in recovery."

"Yes, I'm sure. I just heard the same song and dance from

Robin, but I need something to do. I've consented to stay here with you and Mom while I recover. But quite frankly, I've binge-watched just about all the Netflix I can stand."

"You could catch up on your reading."

"Trust me, I have. And I'll continue to do so. But I'd like to use my brain for something. For something to give back to the medical community. To give back in gratitude for my second chance."

Dad smiles. "I'm not sure I've ever been prouder of you, Raven." Then he frowns. "I shouldn't have said that."

"Why?"

"Because I was most proud of you to see the fight in you when you were sick. The internal strength you had. I'm not sure I could've fought the way you did."

I don't believe my father for a minute. He's the strongest man I know.

Except maybe for Falcon. Falcon, who spent eight years in prison. I was always convinced he wasn't guilty, and according to the conversation I overheard between him and our brothers, I was right.

"I'm glad you're proud of me, no matter the reason."

"I sure am, baby girl. I'll get the name of an attorney for you. It will get this whole process started if you're sure it's what you want."

"I'm sure."

I turn around, ready to leave my father, but then I look over my shoulder. "Daddy?"

"Yes?"

"I love you."

"I love you too, baby girl."

I close the door behind me and leave my father's office.

He's always called me baby girl. Even though I'm twenty-nine years old. Funny that he's never called Robin that. Robin was more like his fourth son than his daughter.

I head to my bedroom to fire up my laptop.

And I see an email that makes me drop my jaw.

4

VINNIE

Anger crawls up the back of my neck. "You're not serious."

Raven Bellamy. I met her only once, and I was struck by her beauty. Even without hair, she rivaled the most gorgeous women in the world.

"Have you ever known me not to be serious?" Grandfather asks.

"That's a little bit of a loaded question, isn't it? I haven't been around the last seventeen years. How should I know what the fuck you are now?" I cross my arms and stare him down. "Although if you want me to take out an innocent young woman—one who just got through hell—you're more evil than I ever thought you were."

Grandfather scowls. "And that's how you speak to me?"

"Sure as hell is." I look around the office. Those art deco paintings on the wall must be worth several hundred thousand dollars each. They're gorgeous, but right now, each priceless square inch of those painted canvases hits me like a tiny poison dart. “What has our family come to? We’re killing for sport now? This isn’t business.”

“Sure it is.”

“Don’t give me that bullshit. Taking out an innocent young woman that has nothing to do with our family is not business.” I draw in a breath. “And I won’t do it.”

“Then I’ll never trust you, and neither will my men.”

“Maybe I don’t trust *you*, old man.” I sear him with my gaze. “Did you ever think of that? I could pull out a Glock right now and put a bullet through your eyeballs. Then I would be in charge, and *I’d* make the rules.”

Grandfather chuckles sardonically. “You’re not armed.”

He’s right. I’m not. No one gets into my grandfather’s office armed. But it wouldn’t take a lot for me to murder my grandfather. I glance around the office. There are lots of objects I could use as weapons—liquor bottles, letter openers, large books. Hell, I could crack his head open with the large brass lamp on his desk. But the most tempting thought is to simply strangle him with my bare hands.

I’m not going to do any of those things. I’m playing a part. Killing my grandfather might stain my reputation with his henchmen. So I take a seat and calmly speak.

“You don’t have to like Falcon Bellamy. But he’s Savannah’s fiancé, and she loves him. And I love her.”

“I love her too.”

I shake my head. “You have a fucked-up way of showing it. These people aren’t involved in our business. Falcon’s not, and his sister sure as hell isn’t. This may not have been the match you wanted for Savannah, but the guy you chose for her is dead.”

“Killed by your father,” he says.

I jump to my feet. "Yeah, killed by my father. You know what? If he hadn't done it, I might've. Rather than see McAllister kill an innocent man—"

"Innocent?" Grandfather scoffs. "The man's an ex-convict. Or have you forgotten?"

"I haven't forgotten anything." I lean forward across the desk, staring my grandfather down. "I got to know him. He's a good man. Did he do what he was accused of? I don't know, and at this point I don't care. He's paid his debt to society, and he's a free man now. And Savannah loves him. That's the end of it. You want me to take someone out who's done our own family wrong? Say the fucking word. I'll do what I have to do to prove my loyalty. But to murder an innocent young woman who hasn't done anything? Whose brother hasn't done anything, other than love my sister? No. It won't happen. Not under my watch."

My grandfather rises slowly. "You're forgetting that this family is still under *my* watch."

"Yeah? Fine. I came back. This is my birthright, Grandfather. You need to start changing with the times. Name a name. Any name—as long as he deserves it. I'll do my duty. I'll kill the motherfucker. But I will never harm an innocent woman. Especially not one who just got a second chance at life."

He stares at me then.

Glares at me.

And I wonder if his eyes are drying out, because he's not blinking.

Despite my urge to, I don't look away. I see this for what it is. It's my grandfather trying to stare me down.

He will look away before I do.

I may have learned to come to peace with my guilt during my time in a Buddhist temple, but I also learned inner strength. I learned the power that you can manifest from within yourself.

Right now, I am taking all that power and focusing it into staring my grandfather down.

I'm not sure how many minutes pass before he finally looks away. "Fine," he says. "The name is Giacomo Puzo."

"Who the hell is he, and what did he do to our family?"

Grandfather sinks down into his leather office chair. "He's trying to nudge into our territory. He's been talking to our suppliers in Mexico, and I don't take kindly to it."

I blink, drawing in a slow breath. "Fine. Giacomo Puzo. I'll take care of it." I turn, walk toward the door.

"Vincent?"

I look over my shoulder, raise my eyebrows.

"I'll need proof."

"Won't his obituary be proof enough?" I ask, resisting an eye roll.

"Bring me his pinky finger. Along with that goddamned gaudy pinky ring he always wears." He wrinkles his nose. "I hate the fucking thing. Does he think he's a goodfella or something?"

"Fine. Consider it done."

I'm not cutting any fingers, but I'll get the fucking ring. That'll be good enough.

I leave the office, walk down the hallway past the reception area and to the elevators. This is my grandfather's front —the legitimate business he hides behind. Bianchi & Sons Imports. We're coffee importers. The finest Arabica beans from Columbia.

It's good stuff. We make a lot of money.

But it pales in comparison to the money we make from drugs.

And now, apparently, people.

A shudder runs down my entire body. What the hell have I gotten myself into?

I steel myself. All part of the plan. I've got to go along with it, just for a while, and when the time is right I'll take it down from the inside. I'll do right by my family.

My real family. Savannah and Michael. My dad and mom. And Falcon, too, I guess.

My grandfather may share his DNA with me, but he sure as hell doesn't count.

Why he decided to branch into human trafficking is beyond me, but we won't be doing it for long.

And Giacomo Puzo?

I won't kill him.

But he'll die one way or another.

~

Puzo is easy enough to locate. He's one of those sleazy two-bit mobsters who thinks he's smarter than he is. He is also an attorney in a downtown law firm. I don't dare go to his place of business. Nope. I need his home address.

My private investigator has a location for me within half an hour.

He runs a drug ring in the back of a dry cleaner in downtown Austin. A gambling ring as well. I could get in the game, but that would be too easy.

I need to talk to the guy first. I can probably make him skip town...but not before I get that damned ring.

I go downstairs and text my driver to bring the car around.

Yeah, I have a car now. A black Mercedes with bulletproof windows. And a driver. His name is Fred. He wears a chauffeur's hat and everything.

I give Fred the address, and forty-five minutes later, we roll into an affluent suburban community to a custom home. The house's façade is a combination of brick and natural stone which is complemented by large, arched windows. A grand double-door entrance is framed by classical columns and topped with an intricate wrought-iron balcony. The roof is adorned with decorous dormer windows, and the walls are lined with climbing ivy.

This is where Giacomo Puzo lives, along with his lovely wife Marinella and their two children, Anna and Paulina.

Marinella and the girls probably have no idea what Daddy does for a living.

Fred parks the car in a circular driveway in front of the home's three-car garage.

My bodyguard, Elmo—yes, that's actually his name—sits beside me in the backseat. When Fred is in front of the house, he moves to get out of the car, but I stop him.

"I'm going up alone."

Elmo frowns. "Mr. Bianchi wouldn't like that."

"Do you think I give a rat's ass what Mr. Bianchi would like? I'm going up there alone. If he's not home, I don't want to alarm his wife or children."

Elmo looks over at the house for a moment, but finally nods. "If you say so, Mr. Gallo."

I get out of the car and take the concrete walkway up to the elegant brick-and-stone two-story. This is a suburban dream. All that's missing is the white picket fence.

I ring the doorbell, and a golden retriever peeks through the side window, his tongue hanging out of his mouth so that he looks like he's smiling.

Man, a golden retriever? Aren't mobsters supposed to have Dobermans or Rottweilers? Who is this guy anyway?

A moment later, a young woman wearing light-yellow yoga pants and a dark-gray hoodie answers the door, shooing the dog out of the way. "Go on, Francis." Then she looks at me. "Hello, can I help you?"

"Are you Marinella Puzo?"

She laughs. "Gosh, no. I'm Clarice, the kids' nanny."

"I see. When do you expect Mrs. Puzo to come home?"

Clarice pulls out her cell phone and checks the time. "Probably pretty soon. She had lunch with the girls, and then a mani-pedi." Clarice rolls her eyes.

I stifle a chuckle. Classic Mafia wife, for sure. "All right. What about Mr. Puzo?"

Clarice frowns. "He works late most nights. I hardly ever see him. By the time he gets home, I've already got the kids in bed and I've retired to my room."

"Oh, you live here?"

"Yes. The nanny position is a live-in job."

I tilt my head. This young woman is being pretty liberal with the information she's giving me. She has no idea who I am. Granted, I'm wearing an Armani suit, and I totally look the part of a businessman. She has no idea I'm here to kill her employer.

Except I'm not going to kill him. Not directly, at least.

I have my own ideas of how to deal with this. I'm not quite sure what I'm going to do, but I'm good at strategizing on the fly.

"Please tell Mrs. Puzo that Vincent Gallo Junior stopped by to see Mr. Puzo."

"Sure, glad to." She smiles. "Do you have a card or something?"

"Of course." I pull my wallet out of my pocket and take out one of my newly minted business cards.

Vincent Gallo Junior, Bianchi & Sons Imports. The Finest Arabica Beans from Colombia.

She grabs the card and reads it. "Oh, I love coffee."

"We only import the best." I give her a quick wink.

I learned while I was in Europe that my good looks can get me pretty much anything I want from a woman. I never took advantage of that, of course.

That is to say, I never used it for the gain of my mafia family. I took plenty of women to my bed, but they had just as good a time as I did.

Unfortunately, I may have to use my powers for evil now.

"It was nice to meet you, Clarice."

"You too, Mr. Gallo."

I dazzle her with my smile once more. "Vinnie. Call me Vinnie."

"Sure. Of course."

I nod and walk away from the Puzo home.

Clarice is a nice girl. Cute, friendly. Clearly overqualified for her job of changing diapers and chauffeuring rugrats to and from their errands.

I almost feel bad about the fact that the man who employs her will soon be six feet under.

5

RAVEN

I can't believe it. It's an email from my old bestie from high school, CJ Simons. She and I haven't talked in ages. Does she even know I had cancer?

How did she get this email?

But I laugh at myself.

My email address is easy.

raven@bellamyranch.com.

I open the email and start to read.

Hey Ray,

Long time no talk! I just wanted to let you know that I'm back in town. I got a cushy job in the suburbs. It's been forever since we've talked. I'm really sorry we lost touch after college. Of course it didn't help that my family moved to Germany and I tagged along. I hope all is good with you, and if you're still around, I'd love to meet up and find out what's been going on with you for the past eight years. Give me a call.

Best, Ceej.

Then her phone number.

CJ Simons.

Damn. We used to hang out all the time. She and I were the only two in the needlecraft club at our small high school.

Robin wouldn't have been caught dead in that club, and frankly, needlecraft wasn't really my thing either, but my mother is excellent at it, and I always loved her work and wanted to be better. CJ's work was always way better than mine. In fact, she used to enter the county fair every year, and she had a stash of blue ribbons in her bedroom at home.

We went to college together as well, and we were roommates all four years.

But no sooner had we graduated when CJ's father, a colonel in the Army, got transferred to Germany, and CJ decided to go with him and her mom. She got a great job as an *au pair* for a German family, and that was the last I heard from her. We emailed for a while, kept in touch on the socials, but then longer and longer periods took place between our emails until eventually it all petered out.

I'm not sure which one of us emailed last.

I start to respond to her when another email pops up on my screen.

I don't recognize the name, but the domain name is one of the law firms my father uses.

I quickly open the email.

Dear Ms. Bellamy,

I'm an attorney at the law firm of Polk and Creighton in Austin. Your father mentioned that you're looking to form a nonprofit. I believe I may be able to help you. Let me know when you're available and we'll set up a meeting.

Sincerely,

Brick Latham.

Brick?

That was my grandfather's name. Brick Bellamy. I didn't know anyone else had that name.

But I'm excited.

My father came through for me more quickly than I thought he would.

I quickly respond.

Dear Mr. Latham,

Thank you so much for your email. My time is flexible, so let me know what's good for you. We can start with a phone or Zoom call. As you may or may not know, I'm recovering from cancer, and though I feel great, my physicians have advised me not to drive for another week or two. After that, though, I'm happy to meet you at your office in Austin. Thank you so much for your offer of help.

Raven Bellamy.

I get ready to email CJ back when I decide to call her instead.

I need to tell her what I've been through and that if she wants to see me, she'll have to come to me, at least for the next week or two.

I punch in the number from her email.

"Hello?"

"Ceej?"

"Oh my God, Raven!"

"Yeah, it's me. I just got your email. So you're back in town?"

"Yeah, I've been back for a couple of months. Unfortunately, Dad passed away, and we had to bring his remains home."

"Oh my God, Ceej, I'm so sorry."

"Yeah, it wasn't pretty. Cancer."

I gulp back my gasp. "How's your mom?"

"She's good. She has an apartment in Austin. It's been hard for her, but she's dealing."

"And how are you doing?"

She sighs. "I'm adjusting. We knew it was coming. It was pancreatic cancer, and there's not much they can do about that. He lived about six months after the diagnosis. All he could talk about was how he wished he had retired ten years ago, once he was eligible. Then he and Mom could've had more time together."

I sigh. I'm not sure what to say. Having been in the situation, I know nothing—no words—can help her.

I could tell her that at least her father had a long life, which he did. Longer than I would've had if Falcon hadn't come through with his bone marrow.

But telling CJ that at least her father had a long life would feel like a punch in the gut to her.

"Raven, you there?"

"Yeah, of course. I'm just so sorry."

"I appreciate that. I'm sorry we lost touch." Her voice brightens up. "So tell me. What's going on with you? I checked you out on social media, but the last time you posted was like three years ago. You're not married?"

Yeah. I've never been much into social media, and once I was diagnosed, I didn't want to post at all.

"No, not yet. I've been...busy."

"And I was always sure that Raven Bellamy would be the first of our group of friends to marry. After all, you were the homecoming queen back in high school."

"True."

"Is that still a sore spot with Robin?"

"Come on, Ceej. It's been a long time now. Robin and I are close. Any drama from high school is long behind us."

"If you didn't look so much alike, no one would even know you were twins. You're so different."

She's not wrong. Robin and I have always been different as night and day. CJ herself was up for homecoming queen as well, as well as Robin, me, and one other girl whose name I can't even remember now.

"So no husband," CJ continues. "Any special man in your life?"

"Not exactly."

"What do you mean *not exactly*?"

"It just means..." I take a slow breath in. "During the last few years I haven't been in a position to really date."

"Okay..."

"It's really something I'd rather talk to you about in person."

"Let's get together then," CJ says. "I'm a nanny to these rich people in this gorgeous suburb. You can come over anytime, because no one's here during the day except me. The kids are in private school, and of course it's my job to take them and pick them up, but the lady of the house is always off doing something. She doesn't work, but she keeps a full schedule. Whether it's a meeting of the Junior League or meeting of the board of something or other from the back-ass of nowhere, you know."

I chuckle at that. "Sounds like a dream job. But...I don't think I can get away. Maybe you could come here?"

"I'm off on Sundays," she says. "I suppose I could. But you know, Ray, it would be much easier if you came to me."

I don't want to tell her about my cancer over the phone, and if I tell her I'm not clear to drive, she'll have questions.

"Oh, come on, Ceej. We can walk through our old stomping grounds. This Sunday?"

"All right, Raven. This Sunday. I just need your address."

"I'm actually staying with my parents right now. My place is being...redecorated."

I hate the lie, but again, I don't want to talk cancer over the phone. When she sees me at the front door with a nearly bald head, she'll realize the truth.

Is it rude of me to not tell her? To surprise her with my bald head?

Well, that's how it's going to be. "Sunday. Come on over around noon. You know my mom always makes a huge lunch on Sundays. It will be great to see you."

"Sounds great, Raven. I'll see you then. And this time, we're not losing touch."

"Absolutely. I can't wait to see you. We've got a lot of catching up to do."

As soon as I end the call, I get another call from a number I don't recognize.

"Hello?"

"Is this Raven?"

"The one and only."

"This is Brick Latham. I'm an attorney in Austin. I assume you got my email?"

"Oh, Mr. Latham. Yes. I emailed you back but maybe you haven't gotten it yet. Thank you for getting back to me so quickly."

He chuckles. "When Austin Bellamy talks, our law firm

listens. I understand you want to talk about starting a nonprofit."

"I do."

"You came to the right place. I've set up many nonprofits here in the state of Texas. I'm definitely your man. We should get together to discuss everything. I can tell you what you'll need so that we can get you incorporated as a nonprofit with the state, and then we'll have to talk about funding and all the other details."

"To be honest, Mr. Latham—"

"Brick, please."

"Okay. Brick. I honestly haven't given the details a whole lot of thought. It's just... I need a project, and this is something that's near and dear to my heart. You probably know that I'm recovering from cancer myself."

"Yes, my partner who referred me did tell me that. And let me tell you that I'm very glad that your prognosis is good."

"Thank you. So am I." I laugh nervously.

"If you can come to the office, I can go through everything with you. We can discuss your idea, and I can help you come up with a business plan."

I sigh.

"Everything okay?"

"Yes, I'm fine. It's just that I haven't been cleared to drive yet. I probably won't be for another week or two, according to my physicians. Don't get me wrong. I feel fine. And I'm sure I *could* drive but—"

"That's not a problem. You listen to your doctors. I can come to you. You name the time and place."

"Great. How about tomorrow? My parents' house."

"Let me just check my calendar." The tapping of his computer keys echoes through the phone. "Looks like I'm available tomorrow morning around ten a.m. Will that work for you?"

"Gee, let me check my calendar..." I let out another nervous chuckle.

"I see. Tomorrow at ten it is then. I look forward to meeting you."

"Me too. Thanks again."

I'm parched after two phone calls. My throat's still a little sore from the virus I just recovered from, so I head down to the kitchen to grab an Orange Crush, my favorite soft drink.

Just as I'm entering, though, I hear my brothers talking.

Again.

"There's one person who may be able to help us," Falcon is saying.

"Who?" From Hawk.

Falcon pauses a moment. "Savannah's brother. Vincent Gallo."

6

VINNIE

Seventeen Years Earlier...

Most guys look forward to their eighteenth birthday.

Being an adult offers new freedoms, new opportunities, a taste of what life is really like beyond the walls of high school and adolescent constraints. But for me, it was more than just a mere transition into adulthood. On my eighteenth birthday, I met with my father and my grandfather to find out what would be expected of me in our "famiglia." We don't use that word anymore. It's simply "family," but I know the origins. I know what it means.

My grandfather, Mario Bianchi, is the head of our family. He fathered only one child—my mother—and married her off to the son of his consigliore, Vincent Gallo Sr.

My father.

I enter the dimly lit study where my grandfather holds court, inhaling the scent of aged leather and cigar smoke. My grandfather is seated behind his grand mahogany desk, a testament to our family's old money. His silver hair is slicked back, and his eyes are hidden behind reading glasses as he examines some papers.

Next to him stands my father, a stark contrast with his brown hair and intense gaze. He is the physical embodiment of power and command. He's been a stern but fair parent to my brother and me. A little softer on our younger sister.

They both look at me. Grandfather sets down his papers and removes his glasses. Father turns toward me and offers a small nod. It's a gesture full of unspoken implications, an acknowledgement that this meeting marks my passage from boyhood to manhood.

"Vinnie," my grandfather begins, "today, you step into a world that demands more than just being an adult. It demands loyalty, honor, and the will to protect our family at all costs."

His words hang heavy in the air. A knot tightens in my stomach, but I keep my gaze steady.

He leans back into his high-backed leather chair. "It's a world that won't tolerate weakness," he says gruffly. "It's a world where men are continuously tested. Failures are costly. Remember, Vinnie, the Bianchis do not fail."

Next to him, Father simply watches, his face unreadable, until he speaks. "Look at me, Vinnie."

I obey, meeting my father's gaze.

"Your grandfather is right, Vinnie," he says. "The world we live in is not for the faint-hearted. You must be strong, steadfast. You must have the stomach for what lies ahead."

He pauses, perhaps giving me time to absorb his words, or perhaps weighing his next ones. Could be either. I don't know.

"There are choices you'll make that will test your mettle, your loyalty, your very soul." Grandfather leans forward, leering at me over his desk. "But remember this. Being a Bianchi is about more than just our name and our wealth. We are leaders, protectors, and, above all, survivors."

His ice-cold stare penetrates my soul as he stands, walks out from behind his desk, and places a firm hand on my shoulder. "Vincent," he says, without looking at my father. "Give us this room."

My father doesn't move.

"Vincent," Grandfather says again, this time his tone more menacing.

My father draws in a breath. "Mario..."

"It must be done, Vincent. Go. I'll not tell you again."

My heart pounds. Why is he making my father leave?

Finally, my father walks toward the door. Without looking back around, he says, his voice grave, "Whatever happens, remember that your mother and I love you very much."

The door clicks shut behind him, leaving my grandfather and me alone in the room. The air between us seems thick, as if a fog has descended from the ceiling.

"Vinnie," Grandfather begins again, his voice gentler now. "There are things you must understand about our family, about our business."

I swallow hard, nodding.

"We are not just businessmen," he continues. "We are guardians of a legacy that spans nearly a century. A legacy built on respect, power, and sometimes violence."

Does he think I'm ignorant?

I'm not.

I know where this is going. I know what's expected of me. I don't like it, but I've accepted my fate.

The knot in my stomach tightens further as Grandfather reaches under his desk and pulls out an ornate box. He places it in front of me on the desk.

"Open it."

I glance at the box, my hand trembling as I reach for the clasp.

The polished wood is cold against my fingertips, and a chill runs down my spine as I pop open the lid.

Inside lies a short, stout stick made of polished wood. It's over a foot in length and the diameter of a broom handle. What the hell?

~

Present Day...

I erase the memory from my mind.

I let it go back in that Buddhist temple.

At least I thought I did. So much else had to go along with it.

But this morning I sat in that same office, facing my grandfather.

And I agreed to end the life of Giacomo Puzo.

What the hell has Giacomo Puzo done to our family to merit this fate? So he's running drugs and gambling. Who cares? I think back to my grandfather's words.

He's trying to nudge into our territory. He's been talking to our suppliers in Mexico, and I don't take kindly to it.

A two-bit mobster is trying to nudge into our territory? He'd be way out of his league.

Doesn't matter. It's business. At least that's what Grandfather would say.

When my grandfather tried to get me to end the life of Raven Bellamy—that beautiful young woman who has already been through so much—I knew what I've always known to be the truth.

He's a ruthless bastard. Evil incarnate.

Killing Raven Bellamy would not be business.

It would be personal. Revenge against Falcon Bellamy for

the death of Miles McAllister and for marrying Savannah, my sister. Savannah is no longer Grandfather's pawn. He can no longer use her to form an alliance.

That's up to me now. I am betrothed to Miles's younger sister, a child of eleven. In seven years, I am bound to take her as my wife.

What my grandfather doesn't know is that by that time, I'll have brought this family down.

If he's still alive by then, he'll be rotting in prison.

But Puzo...

I need to know more.

I can't ask Grandfather. He'll consider that a question of his authority. I have to find out on my own.

Looking into him on my computer will do no good. Everything about him will be above board, of course. Just as everything about the Bianchi family is above board. We're coffee importers. Really rich coffee importers.

Nothing on paper exists about our drug business.

Or about the grisly business of human trafficking that Grandfather is getting into now.

My stomach turns at the thought.

I need to work quickly to take that bastard down before any innocent women and children get hurt.

But while the urgency fuels my determination, it also breeds a necessary patience. Grandfather's empire wasn't built overnight, and I won't be able to destroy it overnight either. If I rush, if I get careless, I could end up in prison with my father.

Despite knowing I'll find nothing of importance, I must start with the web. But not my own computer. I go to the city's public library and find a public computer terminal tucked away in a corner on the third floor. The library is anonymous. No one cares why you're there or what you're looking into.

Giacomo Puzo...

Of Italian descent.

Shocking.

Mid-fifties. Known in the community for his charitable contributions towards building orphanages around the world. Just like us, he appears to be an upstanding citizen.

Married to Marinella Mancetti Puzo, thirty-five, and they have two children, Anna and Paulina, both in private elementary school. Charges of the nanny, Clarice, who I met today.

That has forced marriage written all over it.

But that's not my concern.

Does this man deserve to die?

Because I'll see to his demise if I have to.

Or find a way to fake it.

The computer whirrs softly as I dig deeper into this Giacomo Puzo. Charitable contributions and a seemingly ideal family life aside, there must be something more, something darker lurking beneath the polished surface. Grandfather wouldn't give a damn about some two-bit drug and gambling ring, and I'm seeing no evidence of him trying to nudge into anything of ours.

Dinner parties, benefits, charity auctions—Puzo is a man about the town in the newspaper archives. There's a picture of him at some gala, his arm around Marinella, their faces lit with all the genuine joy of two actors playing a part.

I knew a few Google searches would not be enough. I take a deep breath and look around, making sure I'm not attracting the hawklike gaze of one of the librarians. I reach into my pocket and pull out a small USB stick that contains a portable version of the Tails operating system, which is designed for privacy and security. I insert it into the computer and reboot the system. The familiar library login screen vanishes and is replaced by the Tails interface.

Once Tails is loaded, I open the Tor Browser, the gateway to the dark web. This network is designed to bounce my signal through multiple nodes around the globe to mask my location. I am now a ghost, a digital phantom floating through the encrypted corridors of the dark web.

I'm no stranger to the dark web. I used it almost exclusively while I was overseas, taking care to retain strict anonymity anytime I was online, lest my grandfather figure out where I was and send his goons across the Atlantic to bring me back home—or worse, kill me.

I use the Ahmia search engine to find hidden forums and marketplaces, my fingers dancing across the keyboard as I enter specific terms related to Giacomo Puzo. I'm looking for any hint of personal information—addresses, phone numbers, financial records—anything that could be useful.

After some searching, I find a forum that looks promising, a haven for hackers and data brokers—in other words, a place where stolen information is bought and sold. I register an account using a fake identity and begin to explore the listings. Sure enough, buried within the labyrinth of posts and threads, I find a user claiming to have information on Giacomo Puzo. Probably one of his ex-employees, someone looking to get even after being cut off from the Puzo family.

The seller requires payment in Bitcoin. Again, I expected this. When I was in Europe, I paid for everything in either cash or cryptocurrency. I access my crypto wallet and transfer the required amount. Within minutes, a download link is sent to me. I open it and a file containing the promised information is downloaded to my temporary desktop.

I pore through the information. A lot of things are interesting, but not helpful. I find some medical records—Puzo recently had a colonoscopy, had testicular cancer in his late twenties, and has a pretty serious peanut allergy. I dig a little deeper and find that he's frequented escort services quite a bit in the last few years. Another check for my theory that his marriage is in name only. Compromising information perhaps, but that can't have anything to do with why my grandfather wants him dead.

But then I find something odd, something out of place in this picture-perfect narrative. A strange connection between Giacomo Puzo and an infamous cartel in South America. A too-frequent visitor of a certain coffee plantation, reportedly known as the hub for one of the largest narcotic operations in Colombia.

He's been there often, far too often for it to be casual visits or business trips. Pictures of him with known cartel members —laughing, drinking, living it large.

A sudden wave of nausea hits me as I gaze at a picture dated just two weeks back—Giacomo Puzo and my grandfather sharing a toast, their eyes meeting in a silent understanding.

Why would my grandfather want me to kill his own ally?

That's easy enough to answer. He's not actually an ally.

What I need to know is if this man truly deserves the fate my grandfather has sentenced him to.

I need answers before I can make a decision, so I continue to pore over the archives, hitting every major database, scouring the dark web for even a hint of clarity.

I find a connection between Puzo and a string of mysterious disappearances among the workers at the narcotics operation. But it's not enough concrete evidence to pin him as directly responsible. The missing women and children—was it Puzo's handiwork or a coincidence? Could he be involved with human trafficking? Is that why my grandfather wants him gone? Because he's getting our family into that operation?

With every new piece of information I uncover, it's clear that this rabbit hole goes much deeper than I first thought.

Before leaving, I make sure to cover my tracks. The design of the Tails OS ensures that once the system is shut down, no trace of my activities will remain on the library computer. I close the Tor Browser, remove my USB stick, and shut down the machine, watching as it powers off and reverts to its normal state.

I stand up, glancing around again to ensure no one has been watching me too closely. Nothing to worry about. It's a public library. As long as I'm not jacking off to porn in the corner, the librarians won't care.

It's not until I finally stand up from the computer that I realize how tense the muscles in my body are. I never thought I'd be revisiting the dark web. I thought that once I was back in the States, my time in the shadows of the information superhighway were behind me. I'm so ill at ease that I jerk when my phone buzzes against my pocket with a text.

I take it out, sure that it's some federal employee coming for me for accessing information that was not rightly mine.

But it isn't.

It's Falcon Bellamy, my brother-in-law.

I need your help.

7

RAVEN

I storm into the kitchen. "What the hell is going on here? And don't you fucking dare try to keep me out of it this time."

"Ray..." Hawk eyes me.

"Don't even. If you three are in trouble—"

"Fuck, Raven," Eagle says, his eyes wide. "Anyone can hear you."

"Dad's in his office, and Mom's out."

"There's still the housekeeper," Falcon says. "You need to leave us to this."

"Oh, is that why you're talking in the kitchen, where no one *ever* goes?" I say sarcastically.

"Ray, just go upstairs." Hawk props himself against the fridge, his arms folded across his chest.

"And why should I?" I shoot back. "You lied to me, Hawk. And you never lie."

Hawk rubs his forehead, but he doesn't say anything.

"He didn't lie," Falcon says.

"He did!" I poke Hawk in the chest. Hard. "*He* said

everything was fine, even though I specifically heard otherwise." I turn to Falcon. "I chose to believe you. To believe my brothers. But here you are again, and this time you say you need Savannah's brother to help you?" I shake my head. "Everything is not fine, Falcon. Everything is *not* fine."

Falcon opens his mouth, but I hold up a hand.

"No. Don't go there. Don't play the 'oh, Ray, you're still recovering from cancer' card. I won't put up with it. Something's going on with you three—something that caused you to go to prison, Falcon—and if you don't tell me what it is, I swear to God I'll go straight to Dad."

The room falls into a tense silence, the tick-tock of the kitchen clock loudly echoing. My brothers exchange uneasy glances, their faces etched with conflict and worry.

Eagle finally breaks the silence, his voice unsteady. "There's nothing to tell, Raven. It's just...trivial brother stuff."

"And I'm not part of it?" I snap back, my heart pounding. "You're not even trying to come up with a better lie."

"Raven..." Hawk begins, his gaze softening.

For a moment, I see a trace of regret in his eyes before he retreats behind his usual façade of authority. "It's not that we want to exclude you. It's just..."

"Just what?" The question hangs heavy in the air as I fix each of them with a piercing stare.

Falcon sighs and sinks into a chair, running his hands through his hair. "I'm sorry. But you can't be a part of this. You're better off not knowing."

"I'll be the judge of that." I plunk my ass into the kitchen table chair opposite Falcon. "Start talking or I'm going to Dad."

"Fuck." Eagle runs his fingers through his hair. "Fuck, fuck, fuck!"

My youngest brother is trembling.

He was my baby when we were little. I was his protector. I took care of him while Robbie and the other two boys were out roughhousing.

He's distraught. And I want to help.

Desperately.

"Listen, it's not that we don't trust you." Falcon begins, his voice filled with regret. "It's just that this situation is dangerous."

"And we're trying to protect you." Hawk adds.

"Protect me?" I narrow my eyes at them. "I don't need protection."

"But you do, Ray!" Hawk says, frustration oozing out of him. "Whether you want it or not!"

Silence except for the rustle of leaves against the kitchen window.

"All right," I finally say, my own anger ebbing away in the face of their distress. "If you don't want me to help because you think it's too dangerous, then fine. But at least tell me what's going on."

My brothers look at each other. Finally, Falcon speaks. "We need to go outside."

"Fine by me." I rise and head out the French doors leading to our wraparound redwood deck. In the distance is the pool house.

My brothers follow me out in silence. Falcon steps in front of all of us, hands shoved in his pockets. He looks at Hawk and Eagle, a long look that seems to hold silent communication. They nod back.

"Okay," Falcon begins. "I won't sugarcoat it. We're in deep shit."

I frown at him, but I don't say anything. They're struggling with this, so I'll let them talk at their own pace.

"This has something to do with the time you spent in prison, doesn't it?" I say to Falcon. "I heard that much yesterday. Hawk said you did time for a crime you didn't commit."

He flinches slightly, his eyes drifting from my face over to the horizon. The tension in his shoulders seems to grow even tighter. "Yes," he admits quietly.

"Well, what is it?" I demand.

Eagle starts pacing, biting on the skin around his thumb. It's a habit he developed as a kid when he was nervous or scared or unsure. Seeing him resume such a childhood behavior now unsettles me more than Falcon's admission.

"I always knew you didn't kill that cop," I say. "We all knew it. But you went behind bars anyway. Who the hell were you protecting, Falcon?"

But as Eagle's eyes brim with tears, I realize I already know the answer.

"Oh, E..." I say.

But Falcon's phone interrupts us.

8

VINNIE

"Hey, Vinnie," Falcon says into the phone.

"Hey, got your text. What do you need?"

"Can you come over to my place?"

"Now?"

"Yeah. It's important."

"Is Savannah okay?"

"She's fine. I have a lot to tell her. And you."

"Your text said you needed my help."

"I do." His sigh whooshes into my ear. "I need help with..."

"With what?"

"Just come over. I don't want to say anything more over the phone."

"Yeah, sure. Of course. Whatever you need." I end the call and leave the library quickly, my heart racing.

It's not enough that I have to off some guy. Now I'm getting involved in whatever my brother-in-law is tangled in.

And I don't have a good feeling about it.

In fact, I recall a conversation I had with Falcon when I first returned.

"Did Diego Vega work for your family?" Falcon asks me.

"He did at the time I left," I say.

"If you talk to your father," he says, "you'll probably find out that Diego Vega disappeared about eight years ago. Into thin air. Along with a truckload full of merchandise."

Savannah's eyes go wide. "Falcon?"

"There's a lot more to my story than a young rookie cop getting accidentally killed," Falcon admits.

"Oh my God," she says.

Savannah's mouth is agape, and she's looking at Falcon.

Just what the hell kind of man is my sister involved with?

"Before I go any further," he says, "I need to talk to my brothers."

Fuck.

Diego Vega.

There's a blast from my past, though I didn't say anything to Falcon at the time.

Whatever Falcon needs, though, I'll help if I can. I owe my sister that much.

The drive takes a couple hours, and I leave Fred and Elmo at home. I arrive, pull into the gravel driveway, and walk to the door.

Before I can even knock, Savannah greets me at the door with a hug.

"How are you holding up, Vinnie?" she asks.

If only I could be honest with her. *Gee, Sav, great. Our esteemed grandfather wants me to kill somebody. Some guy who lives in a giant house in the suburbs, has a young nanny, and who apparently is dealing with some drug cartel south of the border. He might also be the reason why we're getting into human trafficking. Oh, and before that? He wanted me to off your sister-in-law. You know, the one who just recovered from cancer.*

Nope, can't say that.

"Good," I say.

She looks at me, raises her eyebrows. "Good?"

"Yeah. I knew what I was getting into."

I did indeed know. I knew seventeen years ago, which is why I left. But that was selfish. So now I'll do anything for my sister. She's the only sibling I have left. I only wish I could turn back time and save Mikey from his fate as well.

"Come on in."

I follow her into Falcon's house. She leads me down into a large family room, where Falcon himself is standing behind the black lacquer bar. His two brothers, Hawk and Eagle, are there. Eagle is looking... Well, I don't know the guy, but he doesn't look good.

But then I drop my jaw.

Sitting in a recliner with a can of Orange Crush is Falcon's sister Raven.

She's so beautiful. And to think... If my grandfather had his way, she'd be dead. Dead, as some kind of warped message to Falcon about interfering with our family.

Not if I have anything to say about it.

I'll kill off all the assholes my grandfather wants me to if it means keeping this woman safe.

Her hair is black peach fuzz, but the lack of hair doesn't make her any less gorgeous. She's tall with dark eyes. No eyebrows or eyelashes, but on her none of that seems to matter.

Her cheeks are rosy, though. Falcon's bone marrow has taken hold, and she's recovering, according to Savannah.

No way would I ever take her life. Hell, I don't want to take *anyone's* life.

"Vinnie," Falcon says from behind the bar. "What's your poison?"

"Scotch. No. Make that bourbon."

"I've got scotch. Some great Macallan twenty-five year."

Fuck. Macallan is my grandfather's favorite. Which means I won't touch the fucking stuff, no matter how much like mother's milk it is.

"Bourbon's good."

Falcon pours me two fingers and hands me a glass. I take a quick sip, letting the smoky liquid slide down my throat. Just the right amount of burn. This is good stuff.

"All right," I say. "What's going on here?"

"You know my brothers, Hawk and Eagle."

Hawk, who looks a lot like Falcon except he's taller and has blue eyes, stands, walks over to me, and shakes my hand. "Good to see you again, Vinnie."

Eagle doesn't rise.

"Eagle," I say.

He raises his head out of his hands, his eyes bloodshot and sunken. "Hey," is all he says.

"I'm sure you didn't ask me here just for a drink." I look at each of them in turn, ending with my sister. "Sav, what's going on?"

Savannah swallows. "To tell the truth, Vinnie, I'm not even sure I know. Raven and I... We're kind of innocent bystanders here."

I turn to my brother-in-law. "What the fuck, Falcon? Are you in some kind of trouble? And you got my sister and yours involved?"

"Savannah will be my wife," he says. "I don't want to have any secrets from her. As for Ray? Well, she was in the wrong place at the wrong time."

This time Raven stands, stalks toward her brother, and sets her can of pop on the bar. "Hey, it's not my fault you guys were talking in our kitchen where anyone could've overheard you."

"You didn't have to threaten to go to Mom and Dad."

Raven turns to face her brother, her dark eyes fiery. But then she softens and places a hand gently on his upper arm. "Look, I get that you saved my life. You know how grateful I am for that. But if you're in trouble, Fal, let me help. You saved my life, and I want you to let me help you with yours."

I can't help staring. Such inner strength emanates from this woman.

"But Raven..." Falcon starts.

She cuts him off with a stern look that could put anyone in their place. "I'm not avoiding the fights anymore, Fal." Her tall figure looms over her brother, even as he stands behind the bar. "I've been on the sidelines long enough. You've all tried to protect me because I was sick. Well, look at me now!"

I do just that.

Who could help but look at her?

The room seems to shrink around her, pulling us into her orbit. Her dark eyes gleam with an intensity that draws me in, makes me feel vulnerable in her presence.

"I almost died," she says quietly after a moment. She returns to the recliner. "You saved me, Fal. But now it's time for me to stand on my own two feet."

Savannah turns to look at me, worry etching lines into her face. But it's not for Raven. It's for Falcon and the potential danger he's in. A knot forms in my stomach. I don't want my sister involved in any of this. Raven either.

Falcon runs a hand through his hair. "Raven, you don't understand—"

"No, *you* don't understand!" she shoots back, standing again. "I'm not your responsibility anymore. I won't let you treat me like a fragile piece of glass."

Hawk sighs. "You're right, Raven. And we're sorry."

Falcon opens his mouth but Hawk holds up a hand.

"You saved her life," Hawk continues. "But we can't keep treating her like she's weak. She can handle herself. We need to trust her."

Eagle, who's been silent until now, rubs his face and nods. "She's here now. Thanks, Ray."

Raven sits down, this time next to Eagle, and grabs his hand.

They're close, maybe closer than Raven is to either Hawk or Falcon. Something's eating at Eagle, and I'm pretty sure it's why we're all here.

"You're right," Falcon finally says. "I just worry about you, Raven."

Raven gives a small smile. "And that's why I love you, big bro. But it's time for me to step up."

Savannah is next to me now, her body trembling slightly as she wraps her arms around herself. She's scared, but she's also relieved. I nod to her, hoping it eases whatever's got her frightened.

"All right," Savannah finally says after a moment of silence. "Now that we have that out of the way, I think it's time we get down to business."

She looks to me, her eyes pleading. Of all the people in this room, she knows I'm the one most versed in the dangerous games our families play.

"Vinnie," she starts, her voice shaky, "Falcon is mixed up in something."

My mind races with possibilities. Drugs, arms dealing, mafia ties? I can deal with that. "What is it?"

Falcon doesn't answer right away. He pours another two fingers of bourbon and downs it in one go before he finally breaks the silence.

"I'm an innocent man," he says.

"I've always known that, Fal," Raven says. "You went to prison to protect someone. I know who, but Vinnie doesn't."

Falcon pours himself another drink, but Savannah walks over to him and pulls the glass away. "Just tell us, babe. Please. You've already done your time, and you protected who you felt you needed to protect. What's going on now? Isn't this finished?"

Hawk draws in a breath. "Unfortunately, no it's not."

I down my drink the way Falcon just downed his. "Maybe you'd better start at the beginning."

"No!" Eagle shouts. "No starting at the beginning. We just need you to get rid of a body, okay? No need to know the details."

Savannah and Raven both gasp in unison, and Raven trembles, still holding onto Eagle.

"See?" Falcon shakes his head. "This is why I didn't want you involved, Ray. This is too much for you."

But Raven looks at her brother, and already I know she's made of sterner stuff. Her body may be weak, but mentally, she's fortitude personified.

Beauty personified as well.

I clear my throat. "I'll hear you out. And I'll help you if I can. But before I do anything—especially getting rid of a body—I want the whole story. You'd best start at the beginning."

9

RAVEN

A new baby.

I'm excited!

I remember a little bit about when Hawk was born, but the memory isn't super clear.

But Mommy and Daddy just left for the hospital. They told me it's going to be another boy.

At first I was disappointed. Robbie already prefers playing with our older brother over me. I like to stay inside and help Mommy in the kitchen, play dress-up with the many princess outfits she's bought me, and hosting pretend tea parties with my stuffed animals. Robbie likes to roughhouse with Fal. Hawk is a little too young right now, but I can tell by how he watches them play that he can't wait until he's big enough to join them. I was hoping Mommy would have another daughter so that I might not be the only girly one.

But after a while, I got excited about having another baby brother. Even if he ends up joining the boys when he's older, for a while he'll be too small. And he'll be mine.

Our nanny got the call this morning. Mommy had the baby

late last night. Daddy is already there, of course, but we're on our way to the hospital to see the baby.

Hawk doesn't really understand why we're going to the hospital. He's too young. And Falcon and Robbie are too busy playing rock-paper-scissors in the car ride over to care.

But I'm sitting there patiently, swinging my little legs over the backseat of our big family car. I picked out my favorite dress to wear today. Pink—of course—with little yellow stars and moons on it. Mommy calls it my princess dress, but the stars and moons make me think of Mickey Mouse in the Sorcerer's Apprentice *cartoon.*

We get to the hospital and rush up to Mommy's room. The fifth floor is where they keep the Mommies who had babies. The boys and Robbie are lagging behind, but I go forward. I'm so excited to meet the baby.

"Ray, please wait up," our nanny says.

But I heard the lady at the front desk. She said Mommy is in Room 520. I'm almost running, looking at the numbers on each door. I finally find it and knock loudly.

The door opens, and a nurse widens her eyes when she sees me. She kneels and smiles. "And who do we have here?"

I twirl my dress. "My name is Raven and I'm here to meet my baby brother."

The nurse laughs. "My goodness. I bet you're excited to be a big sister."

"I'm already a big sister. I have another little brother. But I was really little when he was born so I don't really remember meeting him."

The nurse grabs my hand. "Well, I can tell that little Eagle is lucky to have such a great girl to be his big sister."

I look over at the bed. Mommy's face is dark pink and she's sweaty. But she looks so happy. She's holding a small bundle.

I run in. "Eagle. Is that his name?"

Mommy looks down at me and smiles. "Yes, baby."

Daddy chuckles in the corner. "We're going to have to stop with this one, Star. We're running out of bird names."

I raise my hand. "You could name the next one Big Bird!"

Mommy and Daddy laugh at that. I don't think it's very funny. Big Bird is a great name for a baby.

Daddy walks over to me. "Do you want to meet your baby brother, sweetheart?"

I nod. "Yes, please, Daddy."

Daddy lifts me up and sets me on the bed. I look into the bundle in Mommy's arms.

And I can't help it. I cry.

He's so small. And he's so cute. So precious.

I finally have my own baby.

And I'll make sure nothing bad ever happens to him.

~

GET RID OF A BODY?

Jesus Christ…

What the hell have my brothers gotten into?

My heart is racing as I hold Eagle's hand, but Vinnie? He's holding steady.

Vincent Gallo Jr. has dark hair and eyes that smolder with an intensity that's almost magical. This is a man who left his family, spent over a decade overseas. That's about all I know about him.

I spent so many years fighting for my life that sexual attraction of any kind was a luxury I never thought about.

But looking at Vinnie Gallo now? My libido is back with a vengeance.

He slides a hand through his thick dark hair. The sight would make any woman's heart falter, but for me, it's like a bolt of lightning blasting through my veins and landing right between my thighs.

I clutch Eagle's hand tighter. Vinnie doesn't smile, and I wonder what secrets lie behind those smoldering eyes.

"You sure you're up for this, Ray?" Falcon says. "Because once you know, there's no going back."

I nod slowly. "I know you're innocent, Falcon. But what's the deal with a body? The cop's body was found on our property, shot by your gun. That's old news. What body are you talking about?"

Eagle riffles his fingers through his disheveled black hair. "A different body. The body of a drug dealer," he says. "And it's buried on our land."

Savannah gasps, but Vinnie? His face is like ice. No horror. No surprise. Hardly a reaction at all.

I stare at my older brother. "I was going to ask you to get me another Orange Crush, Fal, but I think maybe I need something stronger."

"Not with the meds you're still on," Falcon says.

He's right. I shouldn't drink. But damn…

I shake my head. "I don't understand. You went to prison for killing a cop. Not some drug lord."

Eagle shakes his head. "Funnily enough, it is possible for more than one person to die at a time—"

Falcon shuts him up with a glare. "Eagle, keep your

damned mouth shut. Leave it to me to explain this to the ladies and Vinnie."

Vinnie stares at Falcon. He's still the best-looking man I've ever seen, but the fact that he didn't gasp like Savannah did has me a little on edge.

So much I don't know.

Part of me wants to go home. To forget everything I heard the guys talking about. Go back to my life of luxury. After all, I'm damned lucky to have a life at all at this point.

I could go home, meet with that lawyer tomorrow, work on setting up my foundation. I could forget all of this.

But there are two things that stop me.

One is my gratitude toward my brother for saving my life. I want to help him if I can.

The other thing?

Vinnie Gallo. His raw intensity. I don't want to leave his presence. I feel a magnetic pull toward him, a force so undeniable and potent that it feels like the universe itself has conspired to bring us together.

I force myself to look away when I realize I'm staring at him.

Funny thing is?

He's staring at me too.

Another good reason to look away. I know I look terrible with my bald head. At least I've put on a few pounds and my complexion is pretty good now. But the hair will take a while to come back.

"Let's all sit down." Falcon moves out from behind the bar and takes a seat next to Savannah on the loveseat. Hawk and Vinnie take recliners.

Vinnie swirls his whiskey in his glass.

"All right," he says. "If you want my help, spill it. Spill it all."

Eagle looks up.

Falcon shoots him a glare. "Hawk and I will tell the story. You stay still."

Eagle bites his lip. "You think I don't know this is all my fault?"

Falcon lifts a hand to shut him up. "Eagle, I went to prison for you. I went to prison because you fucked up. I forgave you, but I can't have you going off halfcocked. *I'm* going to tell the story."

Savannah sits, rubbing her forehead. Falcon takes her hand.

Falcon takes a deep breath in. "Eight years ago, Hawk and I found cocaine stashed in an old barn near the border on the Bellamy property. We didn't know who it belonged to, figured some mule had placed it there and would be back to get it some other time. But we didn't want it on our property, so we brought it home and flushed it."

Hawk darts Eagle a look.

"But then we found out Eagle had stashed it there for a guy he was working for—"

I throw my hand over my mouth. "*What?*"

As much as I love my baby brother, I want to punch his pretty face in.

"Just let me finish. Please, Ray." Falcon rubs his forehead. "Anyway, we found out later that it belonged to—"

"Please don't." Eagle has buried his face in his hands. "I can't relive this."

"You don't have a choice," Hawk says. "We thought this was all buried forever."

"I never meant to hurt anyone," Eagle says.

"We know that," Falcon says. "I didn't have to go to prison for you. That was my choice."

Eagle buries his head in his hands once more.

Vinnie clears his throat. "I think you're going to have to give me the short version. I want to help you, because Sav loves you. But I'm up to my eyeballs in shit with my grandfather. You've got no fucking idea how bad the situation is."

Falcon looks at Vinnie. "I have a feeling I probably do. Let me finish."

I sit, my jaw dropped, as I listen to my brother recount what went on eight years ago.

"We needed cash to pay for the drugs we'd flushed. Otherwise they'd take it out on Eagle's ass." Falcon draws in a breath. "I was the only one who had access to my trust fund at that point, but no way could I get that much cash right away from a bank. You have to put in an order."

My heart drops. "Grandma," I say.

Falcon nods. "Yeah. I went to her. I'm not proud of it."

"She'd do whatever you asked."

"And she did. She gave me the cash. So we made arrangements to meet Vega at the old barn where the drugs had been buried, but Vega didn't show up. At least we thought he hadn't. Two minions did."

"Two big thugs," Hawk says. "You should have seen them, Ray. It was like a movie."

Falcon doesn't react to our brother's attempt to ease the tension of his story. "We stayed in the barn and watched from the doorway as two men got out of the truck. They were thugs, like Hawk said. Muscles on their muscles. Two against three, and we were all armed, but they most likely were too.

We told Eagle to hide in one of the old stalls while Hawk and I took care of things." He glances toward Eagle. "And you should have stayed fucking put."

"Easy, Fal." From Hawk.

"They asked to see Eagle," Falcon continues. "All we wanted to do was give them the loot and get them on their way. But they clearly wanted to give Eagle a once-over. Hawk and I weren't about to let that happen."

"You fucking should have," Eagle mutters.

Falcon glares at our little brother for a moment before continuing. "A minute later, another man got out of the truck. He must have been hiding in the backseat. He was as muscled as the minions, and he wore steel-tipped cowboy boots, jeans, and a black button-down shirt. His features were sharp and pointed."

"Diego Vega," Vinnie says, his voice low, like a growl.

"The one and only," Falcon continues. "He demanded to see Eagle, but we told him no. And then..." Falcon draws in another deep breath, holds it a few seconds before blowing it out. "Eagle comes up behind me and takes my piece."

Eagle whimpers softly, his gaze fixed to the floor.

Again, I want to hold him, tell him everything's okay. But first I want to beat the living shit out of him. What the hell was he thinking?

"We told Vega to just take the money and go, but he said he and Eagle had unfinished business." Falcon swallows. "Eagle drew my gun on Vega, and then both the minions drew theirs on E."

"You two didn't listen to me," Eagle says, shaking his head. "I told you he wouldn't let me out of there alive. That he wanted more than the money."

"For the love of God," Hawk says, "shut the fuck up, E!"

Falcon continues, "I tried to stop you, E, but—"

Eagle lets go of my hand and shoots off the couch. "I shot him! I shot the motherfucker, and I can't say I'm sorry. I'm sorry for the cop. I am. That was an accident. But Diego Vega deserved to die!"

10

VINNIE

I want to be shocked. I want to be as freaked out as Savannah and Raven are right now. Savannah is clinging onto Falcon, and Raven looks equal parts pissed and horrified.

The world isn't mourning the loss of Diego Vega, and I get that Eagle's not sorry. But there's still something that isn't quite gelling with all this.

"Keep going," I say to Falcon, keeping my voice steady.

"Once Vega was dead, the two minions nearly pissed themselves. They ran back to their truck and unloaded a fucking boatload of drugs onto our property. Then they drove off. Last we heard they were apprehended at the border and never heard from again." He swallows and slowly turns his gaze to his youngest brother. "I tried to get my gun back from Eagle, but he was in a trance or something."

"I had just shot someone," Eagle says dryly.

Falcon ignores him. "After the two others drove off, Eagle went running out of the barn, shooting like crazy. He even pointed the gun at me."

Raven gasps. "Eagle!"

"Go easy on him," Falcon says. "He was in shock. Hawk and I got him calmed down and got the gun away from him. We buried Vega and the drug stash under the old barn. At that point we thought it was over."

"Until you found out a cop had been killed," Raven says, her voice cracking.

"Right," Falcon says. "Apparently the cop was out hunting around the edge of our property, and Eagle got him in the shooting spree. Hawk and I made up a story about being out for target practice, and we didn't even know someone had been shot."

"You didn't shoot him," Raven says.

"No," Falcon says. "But my *gun* did. Eagle was only seventeen. I had to take the blame. I don't regret it."

Raven rises then. "I'm leaving."

"You can't leave now, Ray," Hawk says. "You know too much."

"You think I'm any kind of a threat to you?" Raven asks. "I'd give my life for any one of my siblings. I just can't think about all of this right now." She shoots daggers at Eagle with her eyes. "I can't believe what you put Falcon through, Eagle. I don't think I can ever forgive you."

"Raven." Falcon's voice is stern. "Sit down."

"Fuck off, Falcon." She whips out her middle finger toward all three of her brothers. "All of you fuck off."

I look at Raven. All of her. At the anger and fire in her. At her love for all of them. She'll forgive Eagle. She can't not. But she shouldn't be here, and neither should Savannah. "Maybe the ladies should leave."

Savannah crosses her arms. "I'm not leaving."

"Listen, Sav," I say, "if I'm going to help your future husband and his brothers, you may not want to hear what I have to say."

Raven sits then. "I've changed my mind. I'm with Savannah. I'm not going anywhere. The delicate little ladies can stomach anything you big strong men have to say."

"For Christ's sake, Ray, this has nothing to do with your sex," Falcon replies. "We're trying to do you two a favor. If anything goes south, you'll have plausible deniability if you *don't* hear what Vinnie has to say."

Savannah walks up to Falcon, throwing her left hand in his face. "Baby, the second you put this engagement ring on my finger, I was committed to you. You go south, I go south."

"Same goes for me," Raven adds, tapping her hip. "Your bone marrow runs through my body now, Falcon. You're literally a part of me. And I'm sure as hell not going to sit on the sidelines while you figure this shit out."

I say nothing.

I say nothing because I'm not sure what to say. This is a mess.

It's a mess because I *know* Diego Vega. I've known him since I was seventeen and I walked in on my father, grandfather, and Vega when we were still living on Long Island. He wasn't a lower-ranking drug lord then. He was a fucking boss.

And he was scary as hell.

~

It was a rainy afternoon, the kind that seems to drag on forever. The scent of damp earth and cedar wood wafted in through a window left slightly ajar. The men were huddled like vultures around Grandfather's mahogany table. They were talking in hushed tones punctuated by short bursts of laughter. I couldn't make out what they were saying, but I didn't need to. The tension in the room told me everything.

A big boss was here.

Diego Vega had a sort of dangerous charisma about him that managed to both pull you in and put you on edge. His features were sharp and pointed, as if they had been carved from stone by a sculptor inspired by the lethal elegance of a predatory bird, his eyes gleaming with the cold calculating gaze of a hawk ready to strike.

He noticed me then, standing hesitant in the doorway. His lips curled into a grin.

"This must be the little cobra," he said.

"Little cobra?" I asked.

"It's your legacy," Vega said. "Like your father. You should join us."

My father shook his head at me, but I ignored him. I'd be eighteen in a few months. I should know what was going on with us. I wouldn't run away. I was the little cobra, after all, though "little" was hardly a word that could be used to describe my tall stature.

Vega poured me a glass of whiskey, sliding the tumbler toward me. It slid a little too far, toppling over and spilling onto the mahogany.

"Damn it, Vinnie," Grandfather said. "Can't you pay attention?"

I leaned down to pick up the glass. Vega put an arm out to stop me.

"A cobra doesn't pick up after himself." He rang a bell, and one of Grandfather's housekeepers came in. "Susan, can you please clean up this mess?"

Susan nodded timidly. "Yes, Mr. Vega." She grabbed a rag out of her apron and got to work.

Susan was Grandfather's maid, not Vega's. It was a bold move for him to order her around as if she were his own employee.

Susan got to her feet, the empty glass in her hand. At least it didn't break. "Will that be all, Mr. Vega?"

"I don't know." Vega looked to Grandfather. "Will it, Mario?"

Grandfather nodded slowly. "Yes, that will be all, Susan."

"Thank you, sir." Susan placed the empty glass on the counter.

"Good girl." Vega slapped her ass as she scurried out of the room. He poured another glass for me and slid it across the table.

This time I caught it.

Vega grinned. "You are young." He sat back in his chair and steepled his fingers before him like some mob-movie caricature. "But cobras grow."

He looked at me then. Penetrated my gaze, and something rose within me.

"I'm not afraid," I said. My voice didn't waver. I made sure of it.

For a moment, my words hung heavy in the room. Then Vega laughed—a resounding, belly-deep sound that had an edge of menace cloaked in amusement. "So the snake shows his fangs. Good."

My grandfather refilled Vega's glass. Beside him, my father was silent, a muscle pulsing in his temple.

I didn't break eye contact with Vega. His gaze was intense, but I refused to look away. This was a test of some sort—I could sense it—and I would be damned if I failed.

A few heartbeats later, Vega finally leaned back, chuckling as he lifted his refilled whiskey glass. "To the little cobra, then," he said.

I stopped my hand from shaking as I reached for my glass, raised it to the sky with the confidence of a man twice my age.

"Drink," Vega commanded, raising his own glass in a mock toast.

I followed suit, the whiskey burning a path down my throat, its taste sharp and bitter. It was hardly my first taste of alcohol, but it was the first that mattered. This was my first small venture into the family business. My first real taste of it.

Vega looked at me like he wanted to eat me alive. "Cobras have their pride," he said. "And their territory."

My throat tightened. Territory. He was talking about my family. Our home, our business, and our lives. It was a thinly veiled threat. A loaded statement.

Diego Vega was a man to be feared.

I would show no fear.

"My family's territory is not up for negotiation."

"Bold words, little cobra," Vega said. "But bold words need bold actions to back them up."

"I'm ready for it," I replied, willing my voice not to shake.

Both my grandfather and father were glaring at Vega, and truth be told, I couldn't believe they'd let this conversation go on between Vega and me as long as it had.

Vega rose, finishing his whiskey and setting down the glass. "Mario, Vincent"—he turned to me—"little cobra. It's always a pleasure." He lowered his voice. "Remember. Pride comes before a fall."

Once he was gone, the air thinned and I was able to draw a deep breath. "What was that about?" I asked my father and grandfather.

"Just a test," Grandfather said. "One you passed, Vincent. One you passed."

SAVANNAH HAS GONE PALE, and Raven?

Her hands are shaking, but the look on her face is one of quiet countenance. She obeyed her brother. She sat down.

She did not heed my advice, though. She's still here.

I am at once annoyed at her obstinance and impressed—not to mention a little turned on—at her fearlessness.

"I always knew you were innocent, Falcon," she says.

"Listen, Ray," Falcon says. "What you just heard does not leave this room, do you understand?"

"Yes, I understand," she says. "I'm not a fucking moron."

I see her strength again. Inside that body, despite its fragility from her illness and treatment, this woman exudes a strength that I'm not sure her brothers appreciate.

But I appreciate it.

More than I can ever let her know.

"You okay, Sav?" I ask.

"Yeah," my sister finally says. "I knew some of this. I just didn't know the whole story."

Falcon's youngest brother, Eagle, says nothing. Clearly this is something he doesn't allow himself to think about. Perhaps he made peace long ago with the fact that his brother took a fall for him, but now it's dredged up again.

I don't know whether to feel sorry for him or to kick his fucking ass.

I settle for neither.

"So then...what do you need from me?" I ask.

"It's pretty simple," Hawk says. "My father wants to demolish that old barn and excavate that portion of the property. And we all know what he's going to find when he digs through that soil."

"It's been eight years," I say.

"Yeah, but they can still identify Diego Vega from his dental records." Falcon runs his hands over his face. "Plus the drugs are still there. This will all start again. There will be a murder investigation, and again, the bullet inside Vega is from my gun. Shot by Eagle, but my gun."

"I see." A thousand thoughts run through my head.

"What we're thinking," Falcon says, "is that maybe we can get a stay of execution. Have some nonprofit organization file for an EPA assessment or something. Maybe based on the Clean Water Act."

"You got wetlands around that area?" I ask.

Falcon simply sighs.

"If there'd been a problem with the Clean Water Act," I go on, "the barn never would've been built in the first place." I get out my phone and do a quick search. "Looks like the Clean Water Act went into effect in 1972. Do you guys know when the barn was built?"

"Damn," Hawk says. "We'd have to ask Dad."

"Yeah," Falcon says, "and Dad would want to know why we're asking. I suppose we could get the info from City Hall if the proper permits were pulled."

"The place is a wreck," Hawk says. "It's possible it's over fifty years old. Hell, it's possible it's a hundred years old."

"Not a hundred years old, Hawk," Falcon says. "We've got a shot at fifty. Plus with the Clean Water Act being so new, and with Dad's ancestors owning this land since the beginning of time, they could've easily built this barn without even worrying about any federal regulations or local permits." He frowns. "But again, the problem is there aren't any wetlands around that area. At least not that I can see."

"That may not matter," I say.

"No," Falcon says. "Not if you can get some organization to file a lawsuit and hold things up."

I nod. "One thing you guys need to remember. I just got back. I was away for seventeen years, and things have changed since then. Hell, I'd only been brought into the organization for a couple of months before I hightailed it out of here."

"But surely your father—"

I hold up a hand to stop Falcon. "My father's in the slammer, remember?"

Falcon nods. "Yeah. And I'll say again how grateful I am to him for saving my life."

"He did it for me," Savannah says. "All those years, I thought the worst of him when he was trying to get me to marry Miles McAllister. But I should've remembered that he got me out of it not once but twice. And maybe in the end, he just didn't have a choice."

"Well, you got yourself out of that," Falcon says. "You were so brave, Vannah. So brave."

I clear my throat. "When is your father starting the demolition?"

Hawk sighs. "He's already filed the paperwork."

"And how long does that usually take?" I ask.

"Not long for Austin Bellamy." Hawk sighs again.

I draw in a breath. "I'll see what I can do. But damn, I'll have to talk to my grandfather."

"Why should you?" Savannah asks. "Hasn't he given you access to everything?"

"Are you kidding? He's thrilled I'm back, but I was gone for seventeen years, Sav. Mario Bianchi is not going to trust me with everything until I prove myself."

"Then do it without him," Savannah says.

I fix my gaze on my beautiful sister. "I came back for you, Sav. To avenge what Dad and Grandpa were trying to force you into. And to avenge Mikey's death. I want to take down the family, not participate in more breaking of laws."

Savannah's face falls.

Falcon simply nods. "I understand. Your father saved my life. Your family's done enough for me."

"Please, Vinnie!" Savannah bites her lower lip. "I can't lose Falcon. He already gave eight years of his life for something he didn't do. Please!"

"But Falcon didn't shoot the man," I remind them. "And this time, you don't have to take the fall."

Eagle is still trembling on the couch. He's a grown man now, not a scared kid.

Except to his brothers, he's still that same kid.

Probably to Raven as well.

And then I'm surprised as hell when Raven is the one who speaks next.

"I realize I don't have any say here, but my brother saved my life, and I don't want him to go back to prison. And Eagle? Eagle's my baby. He always has been. If there's a way to keep both of them out of prison, please, Mr. Gallo."

Mr. Gallo?

I don't want to hear the name Mr. Gallo from this woman's lips.

I want her to call me Vinnie. Vincent. You fucking stud. Anything but Mr. Gallo. In fact, all I can think about is getting her lips on mine. Such beauty. So beautiful that it's even hard to imagine how much more beautiful she'll be when her hair grows back in. She's a knockout. She could be walking a runway with no hair, and everyone would still think she was the most beautiful woman there.

It hits me then.

I'll do this.

I'll fix this.

I'll fix this for Falcon and his brothers.

I'll fix it for my baby sister.

But mostly?

I'm going to fix it for Raven Bellamy.

I nod solemnly. "All right. I'll do as you ask. I'll figure something out."

Savannah runs into my arms and gives me a kiss on the cheek. "Thank you so much, Vinnie. I know you don't want to break the law, but this is definitely a case where the end justifies the means."

She has no idea what I'm going to do to bring our grandfather down. I talk a good game about not breaking the law, but I'm no saint. And I'm not naïve either. I know I'll have to break a thousand laws before I can bring Mario Bianchi down.

And damn it, the end *does* justify the means.

"I agree with you," I say. "I'll find a way. First thing tomorrow."

After all, this is easy. If I can drink with Diego Vega and look him in the eye before my eighteenth birthday, I can do this. This is nothing.

When Savannah finally lets me go, Raven Bellamy comes toward me and gives me a gentle hug.

My cock responds.

I move away from her, a little embarrassed by my body's reaction.

Embarrassed, but not surprised.

She smiles, and my God she's beautiful. "Yes, thank you. Thank you for everything. Just..." She sniffles. "Thank you."

And in that moment? If Raven Bellamy asked me to end the whole fucking free world, I'd do it.

I hardly know the woman, but one thing is certain.

I will do *anything* for Raven Bellamy.

11

RAVEN

I'm a little taken aback at how Vinnie nudged away from me so quickly.

I hate all of this.

I hate that we're asking Savannah's brother to break the law.

I hate that my brothers broke the law all those years ago.

But I love my brothers.

Eagle has always had a special place in my heart, and now Falcon does as well because he saved me.

And Hawk? He and I have never been that close, but he is still my blood, my brother. Though he has the least to lose in all of this, I want him safe as well.

"Let me get you another drink, Vinnie," Falcon says.

But Vinnie shakes his head. "I need to go."

"Come on. Have you eaten? We can at least feed you."

"I'm good, but thank you for the offer." He turns but then he looks over his shoulder. "I'll be in touch as soon as I have any information."

Then he leaves the room, and Savannah follows him. "I'm just going to see him out."

Alone with my brothers, I place my hands on my hips. "I love each and every one of you guys," I say, "but hear this. This is the one and only time I want you to put that man in a position of doing something like this. He came back to take down his family. Not to participate in its crimes."

Hawk raises his eyebrows. "Ray?"

"You think because I don't know the guy that I don't care? Look, I get what happened all those years ago. And you"—I glare at Falcon—"had no business going to prison." And as angry as I am, I launch myself into his arms. "But thank you," I whisper. "Thank you for protecting Eagle."

Once I let Falcon go, I turn to Eagle. I sit next to him, hug his trembling body. "How did I fail you, E?"

He rubs his eyes. "You didn't."

"I must have. I'm the one who took care of you all those years. When the boys and Robbie were out following Dad around, and Mom was busy running the household. You were my responsibility. You were my baby, Eagle. How did I fail you?"

"You're only four years older than I am, Raven. You weren't my parent. You're my big sister. Sure, you looked after me. But this is not on you."

I kiss the top of his head. "You're clean now, right?"

"Yeah, of course."

But he doesn't look at me. Doesn't meet my gaze.

I look up, meet Hawk's gaze, and then Falcon's. "Is he?"

Neither of them responds.

"Eagle," I say. "Tell me right now. You're clean."

"I am!" He curls his hands into fists. "No matter what the

two of them think. They think I've got something going on. Something with Scarlett Ramsey."

"Scarlett Ramsey?" I wrinkle my forehead. "What the hell does she have to do with any of this?"

Falcon clears his throat. "We don't know. He won't tell us. But you should know, Ray, that he was late getting to the hospital to see you the day of your transplant because of Scarlett Ramsey."

I look at Eagle, but his sad sunken eyes get to my heart.

"You don't know how hard it was for me," he says, "when I found out my bone marrow couldn't save you."

My heart melts.

"We all felt that way," Hawk says. "Especially Robin. She's your twin."

"But I really wanted it to be me," Eagle says. "You know how special you are to me, Raven. And I kind of thought..." He closes his eyes.

I place a hand on his upper arm. "You thought what, E?"

He swallows, his face stiff. "I thought if it could be me who saved you, then maybe my stupid-ass life would actually have some value. Maybe it would make me a little less of a fuck-up."

Hawk scoffs, and I dart him a glare.

I return my gaze to Eagle. "E, you've fucked up. That much is clear. That doesn't make *you* a fuck-up. And you have the rest of your life to make up for what you did. What you put Falcon through." I gesture to my other two brothers. "The three of you need to be a team. We all need to be a team."

"Without Robin?" Hawk says.

"Without Robin." I nod. "At least for now. Why bring her into this?"

"None of us wanted *you* brought into this, Ray," Hawk reminds me.

But then I look again at my youngest brother. "I think I was meant to be brought into this. Eagle needs me. The two of you need me. I'm damned lucky to be alive, and what better thing to do than to help my brothers if they need me?"

Falcon sits down on the other side of me. "Raven, we always need you. You need to look out for yourself right now. You're still recovering."

"Then the three of you shouldn't have been talking where I could hear you." I stand up and pound a fist to my chest. "I may not be able to fix this for you. But I can *be* here for you. I can help you bear the burden."

"That's just it, Ray," Falcon says. "We want you bearing your own burden right now. Healing. Recovering."

I scoff. "I wish you'd quit doing that. You think I can't do both? You think I don't want to help my brothers? I know you think that there's nothing I can do. That I'm not Vinnie Gallo, that I can't go running to my grandfather to fix this. What I *can* do is offer you emotional support. Be there for you the way all of you were there for me when I needed you. When I needed your emotional support when I was sick. When I could barely lift my head. Could barely talk. When my beautiful hair fell out. You were all there for me. You helped me. Now let me help you."

"I'm so sorry, Raven," Eagle says.

"Too little, too late." Hawk lets out a huff.

I glare at Hawk. "Don't think for a minute I'll let Eagle forget his part in this." And I can't help myself. I smack the back of Eagle's head. "That's what I should've done years ago.

I should've known you were in trouble. And if I had, I would've stopped this before it got out of hand."

"We were all gone, Ray," Falcon says. "Don't you think that's haunted Hawk and me over the years?"

"But he's *my* responsibility," I say.

Eagle finally strikes back. "No, Raven. I can't have you putting that on your shoulders. Or the two of you either," he says to Hawk and Falcon. "This was all me. All on me. *I'm* the one who got involved in selling drugs. I'm the one who started *taking* drugs. I was an idiot. The spoiled baby of the family. And I've never even had to pay for it. Falcon paid for my crimes. And now here you all are, trying to help cover up another of my wrongs."

I sigh. "Eagle, I think the whole world knows that Diego Vega is better off dead."

Hawk simply nods.

"I told you once," Falcon says, "that I don't regret what I did for you eight years ago. That I would do it again. But I don't think Hawk or I will be there for you if you fuck up again. So whatever's going on with you and Scarlett Ramsey—"

"Nothing," Eagle says. "Damn it, I don't know how many times I have to say it."

I put my arm around Eagle's shoulders. My baby brother is now so much bigger than I am, the broadest shoulders of our bunch.

"I'm here for you, E. I should've been here for you then. I'm sorry I wasn't, but I'm here for you now. Whatever you need."

"Thanks, sis." He turns me toward him and places his

hands on my upper arms. "But I agree with the others. I want you concentrating on yourself."

"Part of my healing," I tell him, "is being a member of this family again. Focusing on someone other than myself. Trust me. It's what I need."

"All right, Ray," Falcon finally says. "If this is what you need, you do what you feel you can."

"I absolutely will, no matter what any of you say." I hug Eagle, and then I rise. In turn, I look each of my brothers in their eyes. First Hawk, who's still standing, and then Falcon, seated on the couch. Last, my baby brother Eagle.

He nods at me, gives me a slight smile.

The first time I've seen him smile since this all started.

"Now," I say. "We need to trust Vinnie to get done what he can get done. But if he can't? We need a Plan B."

12

VINNIE

I go into Grandfather's office the next morning, determination etched on my face.

"I need some names from you," I say

He raises his eyebrows. "Oh? What names?"

"Anyone you've got in the federal government. Specifically the EPA."

He frowns. "What the hell for?"

"Look. You want me to take over. I'm taking over."

"Really?" he scoffs. "How's Giacomo Puzo doing?"

I strive to keep my face noncommittal. "It's being taken care of."

"I see."

A lightbulb goes off in my head. "Puzo is why I need the Fed connections."

He nods. "I see. So you're going to frame someone in the Feds? Why not just shoot the bastard? It's how it's done."

"I'll be doing things my own way," I say.

He sniffs snidely. "No, Vincent. You'll be doing things *my* way. You think you can waltz back in here after seventeen years and change it all?" He pulls a pistol—complete with a silencer—out of his desk and pushes it toward me. "This is the gun you'll use to kill Puzo. It's unregistered, and I'll know if the bullet came from it."

I shake my head at him slowly. "No."

"Yes." He rises slowly from his chair. "Or do I have to show you how powerful I am once more?"

I laugh at that. A sarcastic chuckle. "I'm not eighteen anymore, Grandfather. I'm thirty-five, and I've seen the world. Probably more than you've ever seen. And trust me. You'll never lay a hand on me again."

"Maybe I won't," he says. "But I've got goons who will."

I scoff again. "Your goons wouldn't dare lay a hand on me. They know who's going to be the boss when you're gone. And quite frankly? I'd be more worried about what I'm going to do to *you* with that gun than what you think I'm going to do to Puzo."

For a split second, my grandfather's face has a look of shock on it.

But he's good.

He hides it quickly.

"You're forgetting who's still in charge here. Everyone's on *my* payroll, not yours."

This time I pick up the gun and point it straight at my grandfather's head.

Again, I see him shudder for a split second. But he's good. He regains his composure quickly.

I gently lay my finger on the trigger. "I could end your life right now. No one would be the wiser. As you say, this gun's unregistered." I frown. "But is it really? Do I trust *you*? You think I need to gain your trust. What about mine? For all I know, this gun *is* registered. Perhaps it's registered to me, and if I shoot you with it, *I'll* go down."

"Perhaps," he replies with a smirk. "But it seems you fail to remember I'm the only one who knows where all the bodies are buried. And let's say even if you do trust this old man and the gun is indeed unregistered, what's your next move? What's your plan after that, Vincent?"

"I've thought about that," I say slowly, lowering the gun back onto his desk. I don't really have a solid plan yet, but I wasn't going to let him see that doubt. After all these years, my poker game has gotten quite good.

"I figured you'd want me to have some grand master plan right away," I continue. "I'll tell you this: it involves not just survival, but growth. And loyalty. Unforced loyalty."

He lets out a rough laugh. "Unforced loyalty? In our business? You've indeed seen the world, boy, but you clearly haven't learned much about human nature from your travels."

His condescension grates on me, his words dripping with a disdain only someone evil could muster. But I hold my temper in check, reminding myself that he is still the one behind the reins.

"Perhaps you're right," I concede. "Perhaps I haven't learned all there is to learn. But I know enough to realize it's time for a paradigm shift within our family. Our business needs to evolve if we want to survive."

He rolls his eyes. "There's no room for evolution in our line of work. You either rule or you're ruled. You feast or you starve. You kill or be killed."

But even as he says this, I can see the weariness in him.

No matter how strongly he projects his outward confidence, he's an old man now. One whose day in the sun has passed.

"Yes, Grandfather," I reply patiently, "and I'm willing to do my part. But right now, I need your connections with the EPA."

"What for?"

"I told you. Puzo."

"Don't underestimate my intelligence, boy. Puzo has nothing to do with the EPA and we both know it. You want this for something personal." He crosses his arms. "We don't *do* personal."

I scoff. A laughing scoff at that. "We don't do personal? Just yesterday you wanted me to kill Raven Bellamy to punish her brother. An innocent young woman who is trying to recover from a catastrophic illness. You don't get more personal than that."

"What do you need the information for?" he demands.

No way am I telling him I need to stop excavation of land so I can recover Diego Vega's dead body from the Bellamy property. My grandfather would find a way to use it against the Bellamys, whether Savannah is engaged to one of them or not.

I grab the gun quickly and retrain at my grandfather's head. "Asked and answered."

"Fine," he says, his voice laced with frustration. "But remember this, Vincent. You're playing a dangerous game. And in our business, you can't afford to lose."

"I don't intend to," I reply, keeping my gaze steady on his.

He gazes back at me for a moment longer before leaning back in his chair and running a hand across his weary face. He takes a deep breath and pulls out a small worn notebook from his desk drawer, flipping it open to reveal page after page of names and numbers. With a heavy sigh, he jots down a few names on a piece of paper and then slides it across the table towards me.

"Here," he says, "These are the people you need."

I take the piece of paper from him, scanning through the names quickly before pocketing it. "Thank you, Grandfather."

"Don't thank me yet," he mumbles, going back to the pile of paperwork on his desk. "You've yet to see the consequences of your choices."

"I can handle them." I place the gun back on his desk and rise.

As I turn to walk away, my grandfather's voice echoes one last time.

"We'll see, Vincent. We'll see."

I exit his office, my heart pounding in my ears. The ghost of his chilling warning lingers, but it's drowned out by the sweet taste of rebellion.

I let out a long sigh, my mind racing with plans and possibilities. I glance at the piece of paper. These are government officials who can be bought. The price will be high, but I will get what I need out of them.

As I stride down the hallway, my shoes clicking against the marble floor, I glance back at the door of my grandfather's office.

I'm doing this for Savannah, for Falcon.

For Raven.

I drive home to my parents' mansion. It's quiet, as only my mother, the housekeeper, and I live here now.

I head to the room that once housed my father's home

office. It's mine now. Once inside, I shut the door and lean against it, letting out a breath I didn't realize I've been holding. The paper feels heavy in my pocket—heavy with the potential for chaos.

I pull it out and stare at the hastily scribbled names again. There are three—a senator from Louisiana, an EPA chief, and a city councilwoman from New York City.

I text the EPA chief from a burner phone. She's the one I need, after all.

The response is swift, a short and simple *Yes?*

I take a moment to consider my words, knowing that they carry great weight. This is a person Grandfather—and probably my father as well—has had dealings with.

I type out my message.

Need a favor. Confidential.

Her reply is almost immediate. *Who is this?*

I smirk at the screen. She isn't playing games.

A mutual friend, I reply.

A pause before she replies again.

What kind of favor?

The kind that requires your professional involvement and discretion.

Another pause—longer this time—before she finally sends back a single word.

Details.

I text back. *Need an EPA stay on some private property near the Texas border.*

A moment passes before the three dots appear to move. I wait for her response.

The Bellamy property?

My heart races. She knows?

Fuck. I'm in now.

Yes, I text back.

Another long pause.

Wheels are already in motion, she finally replies.

I stare at the screen, mind whirling. What does she mean by that? Is she with me or against me?

Clarify, I type back, my fingers shaking just slightly.

The damnable ellipsis appears again, taunting me as I wait for her response.

The dilapidated barn by the border. It's a high-risk zone. Paperwork has been filed. Bellamy will be notified first thing tomorrow not to begin excavation.

A high-risk zone? My heart thumps. Tomorrow? That's much faster than I anticipated. This is real. *Real.*

I'm in this. I knew I was, but now it's certain. I'm using my grandfather's nefarious contacts to help a friend. It's personal. We don't do personal.

Thanks, I text, trying to maintain an air of calmness despite the panic bubbling up inside me.

Don't thank me yet, she messages back, eerily echoing my grandfather's words from earlier.

I place the burner phone down on the desk.

Someone got to her before I did.

It wasn't the Bellamys.

And it wasn't me.

Who the fuck else knows about this?

13

RAVEN

Dad lets me use his office for the meeting with the attorney today.

I'm more than a little freaked about what I learned from my brothers yesterday, but I use my desire to give back to the medical community to keep my mind at bay.

I'm going to start a nonprofit organization to benefit the research and treatment of blood cancers.

It's what I feel called to do. After all, I'm lucky to be alive.

Our housekeeper shows the attorney to the office where I'm sitting behind Dad's desk.

The attorney, a handsome man with a chiseled jawline and wearing a tailored suit, strides in. He looks professional, yet his eyes hold a touch of warmth that soothes my anxiety. He takes the seat across from me, his briefcase resting on his knees.

I rise. "You must be Mr. Latham."

"Yes, I'm Brick Latham, and you of course are Raven Bellamy."

I nod, taking a deep breath. I straighten my spine and meet his gaze. I'm nervous, yes, but this is important.

"I want to start a nonprofit organization," I say, my voice steady. "For blood cancer research and treatment."

Of course Latham already knows this. We spoke on the phone. He opens his briefcase to take out some documents. "Very well," he says. "We have quite a bit of paperwork to go through." He leans forward. "Blood cancer research and treatment is a wonderful initiative, Ms. Bellamy."

"Please, call me Raven," I say.

His eyes brighten. "Of course, Raven." He returns his attention to his materials. "Starting a nonprofit involves several key steps. Let's break it down. The first thing you need to do is to clarify your mission. What specific support services and resources are you planning to offer?"

I nod, smiling. I've thought this through a bit since last night. "I think I'd like to arrange support groups for emotional support, raise money to allow patients to apply for financial assistance, and champion awareness campaigns."

"That's a comprehensive mission." Brick jots down a few notes on a legal pad. "The next step is to form a board of directors. This group will guide the organization and ensure it stays true to its mission. Do you have people in mind who might join your board?"

"I've talked to my sister, Robin, about being on the board."

He nods. "Anyone else?"

I scratch my chin. "Not really. But I'm sure my parents would be interested."

"Perhaps someone who isn't related to you?"

My mind immediately goes to Vinnie. I barely know the man, but I can't shake the feeling that he would be a passionate advocate for my cause. But his hands are full with both the business of his family and now the mess my brothers are in.

I twiddle my fingers. "I'm sure there are some doctors at the hospital who would be interested. They would also provide some important insight from their perspective. And I've recently reconnected with a college friend, CJ. Her father just passed away from cancer, so I imagine she would be interested."

"Great. It's important to have a diverse and committed board." Brick leans back slightly, his gaze matching mine. "The specifics will come with time after you've talked to some potential members."

"I'll make time to gauge interest among the community."

"That'll be great." Brick smiles. "After forming your board, you need to draft your nonprofit's bylaws. These are the rules that will govern how your organization operates. I can help you with this, but you might also want to consider consulting with other experts in nonprofit law. They can even give you some templates to look at if you're at a complete loss of where to begin."

I realize I should be taking notes as well. I grab my phone. "I'm not texting, I promise you. Just want to write all of this down. What comes after the bylaws?"

Brick's smile widens. "The next step is to incorporate your nonprofit. This involves filing articles of incorporation with the Texas Secretary of State office. That will include your nonprofit's name, purpose, and the names of your board members, so you'll need to solidify all of those. I can help you with the nitty-gritty of what Texas specifically requires."

"Is there anything specific we need to include in the articles of incorporation?"

"Yes." He leans a little closer. "You need to ensure that your articles of incorporation include specific language required by the IRS if you plan to apply for 501(c)(3) tax-exempt status. This includes a statement of purpose that aligns with IRS requirements and a clause dedicating your assets to another 501(c)(3) organization if your nonprofit dissolves."

"Whoa. Slow down." I tap away. "Five-oh-one-see-three?"

"That's the IRS designation for nonprofits organizations. That'll ensure that you don't have to pay taxes on any donations you receive. All of the money will go toward your mission. And because it isn't a for-profit business, you don't have to worry about investors or anything like that. Just throw a gala or two each year to keep your donors happy."

I nod. "Got it. And once we've incorporated?"

Brick looks down at the documents in front of him. There's a small patch of pink in his cheeks. "After incorporation, you need to obtain an Employer Identification Number, or EIN, from the IRS. This is like a Social Security number for your organization. You'll need it for tax filings and opening a bank account."

"Okay, I'll make sure to do that." I tap the letters *EIN* into my Notes app. "And how do we go about getting tax-exempt status?"

He pushes a sheet of paper toward me. "You'll need to complete and submit IRS Form 1023. There's a long form and a short form depending on the size and scope of your nonprofit. The application process can be detailed, so it's often beneficial to work with someone experienced in nonprofit law to ensure your application is complete and accurate."

I smile at him. "Good thing I've got you to help me, Brick."

Brick scratches his arm, his eyes warm and soft. "I'm more than happy to help you through all of this, Raven. It's a noble cause, one that I'm honored to assist you in."

My cheeks warm at his words. "Thank you. I'm just trying to make my second chance at life count for something."

He nods. "You are wise beyond your years." His gaze lingers on mine for a moment, but then he sharply cuts away and looks down at the table. "There are a few more things you'll want to do. You'll need to register for state and local taxes, and you may need to apply for a charitable solicitation license if you plan to raise funds publicly. Additionally, developing a strong fundraising plan and a strategic plan for your programs will be essential for your nonprofit's success."

"And you'll help me with all of that?"

Brick adjusts his tie. "Like I said, it would be my honor."

I tap a few more words into my notes and then put my phone down. "Thank you so much for all of this. It's clear I've got a lot on my plate, but I'm determined to get this done and make a difference." I stand up and reach my arm out. "Would you like to join me for lunch? It's the least I can do for all your help."

He stands up and shakes my hand quite tenderly. "I would be delighted, Raven."

We head into the kitchen. The housekeeper has prepared some ham and cheese sandwiches.

"How have you been feeling since your treatment ended?" Brick looks me up and down. "You look fantastic."

I absentmindedly run my fingers over the small growth of hair on my scalp. "You're joking. With this peach fuzz?"

Brick smiles. "A lot of women cut their hair short nowadays. I think it's quite fetching." He widens his eyes. "I apologize. I'm not sure that was an appropriate thing to say to a client."

I chuckle. "I've felt like absolute shit the last couple years, Brick. I'll take a compliment on my looks any day."

Brick inches his hand closer to mine across the table. "I don't think I'll find any shortage of compliments on your appearance, Raven."

My cheeks are quite warm now. But not as hot as they feel when I'm within twenty feet of Vinnie Gallo. "You're flattering me. I am happy that my face is filling out again. I was looking pretty gaunt during the worst parts of my treatment."

Brick nods. "I can't even begin to imagine what you've been through. You're very brave. And your first thought upon completing your treatment is how you can help others who are less fortunate than you."

I swallow. "It just feels like the right thing to do."

We return to our work after lunch. Brick helps me fill out the nonprofit IRS form, and we spend some time revising the draft mission statement several times until we're both satisfied with it. After another hour, Brick gathers the documents and his notes and stacks them together neatly.

"You've done incredibly well," he says. "This might seem daunting now, but trust me, this is just the start." He tucks the papers into his briefcase. "It's been a pleasure, Raven."

For the first time, I notice a dimple on the left side of his chin. It's unusual...and very attractive.

He clears his throat. “Would you perhaps want to discuss this further?”

I’m exhausted, and really, what more is there to discuss at this point? We got a lot done in this session, and Brick was extremely helpful, but I have a lot of work to do before we’re started. “Of course. Next week maybe, once I have the chance to work out the business plan and all.”

Brick smiles. “That was my failed attempt to ask you to have dinner with me, Raven.”

I stop my jaw from dropping as my hand wanders back to my peach-fuzz head. It was one thing for him to compliment me on my appearance, but now he’s asking me out?

Me?

A woman who’s still practically bald from cancer treatment?

Granted, I’m recovering well thanks to Falcon’s bone marrow, and I’m excited about this new project, but…

A handsome lawyer is asking me out?

My surprise must be evident, because his smile fades slightly. “I understand if you’re not interested, or if you—”

“No,” I interrupt, shaking my head. “I mean, yes. I mean, I’d love to have dinner with you. I’m just…surprised.”

He chuckles. It’s a low, warm sound that fills the room. “Surprised? And here I was worried you’d forgotten that you’re an incredibly strong and beautiful woman.”

My cheeks warm once more at his words. I’ve been so focused on my recovery and the nonprofit organization that I’ve forgotten to let myself live a little.

“All right then,” he says. “How about this Friday at seven? There’s a quiet Italian place about thirty minutes from here.”

He’ll have to drive here from Austin to get me. It’s a long

way. I open my mouth to voice this thought, but then close it. He knows that. He did it this morning. Why bring it up?

"That sounds lovely," I reply, warmth flooding my cheeks once again.

The dimple in his chin winks at me as he stands up to leave. "Until Friday then," he says, extending a hand. "I'll pick you up here, if that's all right?"

"Yes, that's fine."

"Good," he says with a nod. He looks ready to turn away, but then pauses to meet my gaze once more. His eyes are warm, genuine—different from the professional lawyer I met hours ago. "And Raven?"

"Yes?"

"Just because you're on a mission doesn't mean you can't enjoy life. Remember to take breaks now and then." His smile is caring, almost tender.

I take in his words. "Thank you, Brick."

I see him to the door and then go back into Dad's office. I lean back into the chair and let out a breath. The road ahead is long and filled with challenges, but for the first time in a very long while, I feel truly alive. I have a purpose—to help those battling blood cancers, save lives like mine was saved by my brother.

And I have a date.

A date!

But one thing nudges the back of my neck.

I wish the date were with a handsome man named Vinnie Gallo.

14

VINNIE

My phone rings the next morning right as I'm about to leave to see Grandfather.

"Yeah?"

"It's Falcon Bellamy."

"Hell, I didn't even look. I was just going to call you."

"I just wanted to thank you," he says. "Dad got served with the EPA papers early this morning. He can't do anything until the EPA comes out and assesses the situation, and then they'll decide whether he needs to do an Environment Assessment or an Environmental Impact Statement."

Fuck. Do I tell him it wasn't me? Or do I let him think I worked a damned miracle?

This is Savannah's fiancé. I can't lie to him.

"I got the name of an EPA chief from my grandfather, one Myra Pearson. I had instructions to text her at a number from a burner phone, which I did."

"Whatever you did, it sure worked."

"Listen," I say. "I don't want to be presumptuous or anything, but can I come over to your house for dinner?"

"Well, sure, if you want. You're always welcome here, Vinnie."

"I don't want to talk about this over the phone, not until… Let's just talk tonight."

"Savannah already invited Raven for dinner."

"That's no problem. She knows everything anyway."

Plus my heart is racing at the thought of seeing her again.

Man… I haven't had a reaction like that to a woman in a long time.

I need to nip it in the bud, though. I can't drag Raven Bellamy—or anyone else—into the hell that is my life right now.

"Six thirty then," Falcon says.

"I'll be there."

Driving to Summer Creek, when I was just there two days ago, wasn't something I'd planned on, but I can't get it out of my head that someone is watching. Hell, I know my grandfather is watching me. That's a given. But someone else is as well. Someone's watching me. Or Falcon and Savannah. Or all of us.

I can feel it.

Who would be that interested in Falcon and Savannah? We've already made peace with the McAllisters after I agreed to marry Declan McAllister's daughter Belinda when she comes of age. Of course, they lost their son, but my father's rotting in prison for the deed. Miles McAllister was also about to shoot Falcon in the head when my father took things into his own hands, so I'm certainly not mourning his loss.

I'm thankful that he's dead. Savannah's happiness means more to me than my own.

If only I'd been thinking about her and Mikey instead of

myself when I abandoned them. Savannah was only ten years old when I left.

When I left the family at eighteen, we were still living on Long Island. But as I drive through these Texas roads for the second time in forty-eight hours—again without Fred and Elmo—I realize how beautiful it is here.

The colors of the setting sun streak across the sky, their hues reflected in the mirror-like surface of the creeks dotting the landscape. The marsh-green grasslands stretch out like an unending blanket.

A few lone ranches break up the rustic landscape, nestled among groves of Texan live oak. The air smells clean, fresh and earthy—a far cry from the heavy industrial scent that clung to Long Island.

Lost in my thoughts, I almost miss the turnoff to Falcon's place. I pull into his driveway, a gravel path leading up to a ranch-style house with big windows overlooking the creek behind it. As I step out of my vehicle, I hear laughter echoing from inside.

Savannah's voice. And the voice of Raven, a beautiful tone that has somehow become ingrained into my mind.

They're laughing.

They're happy because they think I did the impossible.

When in fact I had nothing to do with it. A fact I need to tell them all now.

I walk up the pathway and knock on the door, and their two dogs, Sydney and Sammy, bark, tails wagging.

Savannah opens the door, shooing them away. "Vinnie!" She throws her arms around me.

"Hey, Sav."

"Falcon's down in the family room. Go on down and he'll get you a drink. Raven's just helping me in the kitchen."

"Hi, Vinnie!" Raven calls from the large kitchen.

"Hi there," I say, my voice cracking a bit.

For the love of God. I'm thirty-five years old. Why is my voice cracking when I talk to a woman?

I certainly wasn't celibate when I was in Europe. A small portion of that time I spent in a Buddhist temple. The rest? I fucked my way around Europe...and did a few other things I'm not proud of.

Savannah walks back to the kitchen, looking over her shoulder at me. "I hope you like lasagna, Vinnie."

Wow. I really have been gone a long time. How could Savannah not remember that lasagna is my favorite?

We had a housekeeper while we were growing up—I think her name was Serafina—and she made the most amazing lasagna. Nothing I had in Italy was as good.

"Love it," I reply, and then I make my way through the hallway and down the few stairs into

Falcon and Savannah's family room.

This family room, where only two days ago, I learned the whole story.

Falcon smiles from behind the bar. "Bourbon?"

"Got anything stronger?"

"Scotch?"

Scotch isn't exactly stronger than bourbon, but it burns my throat like nothing else. I don't care if it's my grandfather's favorite. It's what I need at the moment. "Scotch sounds great."

Falcon pours me a couple fingers, and I down them in one

swallow. The smoky, peaty taste claws down my throat like acid.

Perfect.

But Falcon is eyeing me. "You doing okay?"

I wipe a few drops of Scotch off my lips. "I need to talk to you."

"Do I need another drink?"

I shake my head. "I think you need your wits about you, and so do I. But I'll take another Scotch, this time with a touch of soda."

Falcon mixes my drink, his jaw rigid and tense. "Do I need to call the ladies down here?"

"No." I look back toward the kitchen and lower my voice. "Not that we need to have any secrets from them. I mean, they both know everything anyway. But I don't want to worry them if there's no need to."

Falcon narrows his eyes. "But you're worried about something."

"I'm not sure if I *need* to be worried yet," I tell him.

"Lay your cards on the table, Vinnie. It's always best that way."

I nod and take a sip of my drink. "I got a name from my grandfather, like I told you. One of the EPA chiefs who has worked with our family in the past. I texted her, following the instructions from my grandfather, told her what we needed." I lean toward Falcon. "And get this. It was already in the works."

Falcon drops his jaw. "I guess we don't need a plan B after all."

"Yeah. I was as surprised as you are." I look directly into

his eyes. "Think hard, Falcon. Does anybody else know about this?"

"No." He rubs at his forehead. "Well... There were those two goons. We were all really surprised that Diego Vega himself showed up."

"Yeah, I thought that was weird myself," I say. "He must have gotten demoted. The first time I met him, he was a major crime lord. A kingpin." I take another drink. "But a major crime lord wouldn't concern himself with a paltry million bucks and a kid who got in over his head."

"I wouldn't know if he was demoted." Falcon presses his lips together. "But your grandfather would."

"Yeah, he probably would." I sigh out a deep breath. "I haven't had the presence of mind to ask him. I don't want to bring up Diego Vega to him. I don't want to implicate you in any way."

"I didn't go to prison for killing Diego Vega, Vinnie. I went to prison for killing that young cop, Jaden Perez."

I nod, taking another drink. "Yeah, I know that. But hasn't anyone put two and two together? That Diego Vega disappeared right around that same time?"

"Not that I'm aware of."

"And the two goons." I scratch the side of my head. "You say they got stopped at the border and no one ever heard from them again."

Falcon nods.

"I think those might be what we call loose ends, Falcon."

Falcon widens his eyes. "You think they're still around? And are looking for Vega?"

"Hell, no. My guess is Vega probably treated them like

pieces of shit and they're happy he's gone. But they *are* loose ends. Do you happen to remember their names?"

Falcon shakes his head, scowling. "Never got their names. Never wanted their names."

"Would anybody know?"

"Maybe Eagle. I mean, he was working with them." Falcon rakes his fingers through his hair. "But damn. He's already a fucked-up mess."

I want to tell him that I agree, but I'm not going to talk shit about someone in his family. I simply nod. "Got it. But we need to get him back over here."

"Savannah was looking forward to having a nice dinner with Raven tonight." He glances back toward the kitchen, frowning. "The two of them think this is all taken care of."

"It may be," I say. "The fact of the matter is that I don't know, Falcon. But someone alerted this woman—someone who no doubt knows she's on the take—that we needed someone to intervene on your father digging up that property. Who else would have any interest?"

"I don't know... The EPA itself? Maybe there really *are* wetlands there?"

I take one more drink, letting it soothe my throat. "That's a possibility. But only a possibility. Certainly not a probability. Are you sure no one else knows that Vega was there that night?"

"No one could, other than the two goons."

"Then it's got to be them. If it's not? We've got an even *bigger* problem."

"Yeah," he says.

"I'll try to find them," I tell him. "I've got all my grandfather's resources, and they can be found. But it won't happen quickly. And if it's someone other than those two? We'll be looking for a fucking needle in a haystack."

15

RAVEN

I open the oven to check the lasagna and inhale the robust scent of the tomatoes and cheese. "It's bubbling nicely."

"Great," Savannah says. "We just need to give it about ten more minutes. Turn on the broiler so it gets nice and crusty on top."

I do as she asks, and then I inhale again. "Food tastes so good now. It's richer, creamier, sweeter, more savory. Everything is. You name it."

Savannah smiles. "I suppose it would after not having an appetite for so long."

"Yeah, that too."

She wrinkles her forehead. "That too?"

"Yeah." I purse my lips. "I guess it's hard to explain if you haven't spent the last couple years believing you were going to die."

Savannah nods. "Oh, I know what you mean. Like the sky is bluer now and all that."

"Yeah, exactly."

"I can't say I've been through what you've been through," she says. "I would never attempt to say I understand." She draws in a deep breath, her face suddenly grave. "But I *have* looked my mortality in the eye. Or at least my life as I knew it. When Miles McAllister locked me in his bedroom and was getting ready to rape me."

An anvil sinks in my gut. Right. Just because someone hasn't experienced cancer specifically doesn't mean they can't empathize with what I've gone through.

Savannah has faced her own mortality. I'm sure Falcon did many times when he was behind bars. Certainly Eagle has too, though most of that was his own damned fault. Hawk is a closed book, but I'm sure he's had struggles.

I'll keep that in mind going forward. Everyone has shit they've dealt with. How much it stinks changes from person to person, but the smell is still there.

I turn to Savannah, lay a hand on her upper arm. "You're very strong, Savannah. I'm impressed that you figured a way out of that yourself."

She cracks a small smile. "Are you kidding me? I didn't do anything. I guess the sight of him just made me so sick that I threw up. Projectile vomited all over him and myself."

I must make a face in reaction to what she said, because she quickly widens her eyes. "Sorry. That's not exactly an appropriate topic of conversation when we're preparing dinner."

I chuckle. "Savannah, you never have to apologize. I puked my brains out when I was doing chemo. I'm completely and fully desensitized to the subject."

Savannah wrinkles her nose, but I can see a hint of a smile in her eyes. I know what's going through her mind. I've seen the same look on the face of each member of my family. She wants to playfully return my joke about my illness but doesn't feel it's her place.

"Well, it was enough to get him off me, and then I was able to escape." Her face darkens. "But if Falcon and his buddy hadn't come after me, I'd still be there. He would've found me eventually."

"Seems we both owe our lives to Falcon," I say with a smile.

She smiles back at me. I really like my new sister-in-law. Falcon made a good choice in her, and I want my brother to be happy. He already lost eight years of his life trying to protect one of us. And then he gave me his bone marrow and saved me. He saved Eagle's life and mine, and now Savannah's as well.

I owe everything to my big brother.

"He certainly changed my life," Savannah agrees. "I never thought I would fall for an ex-con. Certainly not one who was assigned as my parolee."

"Do you miss working as a parole officer?"

She frowns. "No, not really. It wasn't my choice. My original choice was to go to law school, but that didn't work out. My father decided after college I was going to marry Miles McAllister. I got out of it by agreeing to go work in one of the parole offices in Austin. I had to do what they asked when they came to me."

My heart breaks for her. "So you basically had to break the law for them."

"I forced myself to think of it only as *bending* the law," she says. "It was the only way I could live with myself."

"But you truly wanted to be a lawyer?"

"That was what I always wanted to do." She inhales slowly and sighs. "But you have to understand that in my family, careers for women are frowned upon. I mean, in a family where they basically sell off their women as brides to form alliances... Well, you can imagine."

"How did you manage to get as far as you did then?"

"My father had some different ideas. He taught me how to handle a gun, for example. And he made sure I was allowed to go to college, if not law school."

I shake my head. "I can't even imagine. My parents always treated Robin and me the same as the boys. In fact, for the first ten years of our life, Robin was convinced she *was* a boy."

"And you?"

I shrug. "I was never the outdoorsy type like she and the boys were. Don't get me wrong. I know my way around the ranch. I learned to ride a horse and how to take care of livestock and everything else we do. It was a requirement from both my parents. But I tended to have more interest in what Mom did. Taking care of the home, cooking, and baking. Just more of what I enjoyed, to be honest."

"There's nothing wrong with that."

"I guess I'd make a darned good mafia wife." I force out a chuckle.

Savannah raises her eyebrow. "You, Raven, would make a terrible mafia wife."

"I was kidding, Savannah."

Her cheeks redden. "I figured as much. It's just that... Just because you're interested in more traditionally feminine things doesn't mean..." She exhales sharply through her nose. "What I'm trying to say is you're one of the strongest people I've ever met. You think for yourself. You have no qualms about making your opinion known. The mafia dons don't really like those qualities in their wives."

I smile, but then I cast my gaze to the kitchen tiles. "I consider myself strong, but not for the reasons you may be thinking. Sure, I got through cancer. You do what you have to do." I sigh. "So many people aren't as lucky as I was. When you look your life in the eye, you realize you'll do anything—and I mean anything—to live. You let them pump poison into your veins so that all your hair falls out and you feel like complete shit. And I wasn't kidding about the puking. You vomit all the bile up from your stomach, cramping because the heaves are so hard. You watch the fat dissolve from your body, and you stop getting your period. But you do it. You do it all for that next breath of air."

Savannah frowns. "You don't consider that the reason why you're strong?"

"I'm saying that you would do the same thing. Anyone would. Unless you're suicidal, the will to live is strong in everyone, Savannah. And I guess you don't know that until you've looked your life in the eye."

"Yeah," she says. "I do get it. Miles wasn't going to kill me, but he was going to rape me. Pretty much make me his. So I kind of get it. Plus...there have been other times..."

I simply nod. Falcon has told me more of the story of him and Savannah. About how she was being hunted by two of her family's goons, how she defended herself with a few pieces of broken mirror when she realized they had come for her.

How she hid out in the safehouse with Falcon for several weeks, not knowing when that awful family would finally find her.

And she did put her life on the line in a way. She wouldn't have literally died if she had married Miles McAllister, but she was giving up her freedom, not to mention the love of her life. She was willing to sacrifice her own identity, her sense of self.

Is that really all that different from simply dying? In many ways, dying would be the easier way out.

I shake the thought out of my head and return my focus to Savannah. "Do you think you'll go back to work?"

"As a parole officer?" She shakes her head. "No. There were aspects of it that I enjoyed, but it was never my dream."

"What about law school?"

"I've considered it," Savannah says. "But right now, everything is on hold."

"Yeah, I can understand that."

"But maybe someday," she says. "I'm still pretty young. I could have a career as a lawyer if I want. But I think I might also want children. And that's something Falcon and I haven't really discussed."

"I think you'll both make great parents," I say.

She grins. "I think we would too. But like I said... It's on hold for now. Until... You know."

I nod.

"So how's everything going with you?" she asks me. "You met with that lawyer today, right?"

"Yesterday, actually." My cheeks warm. "You won't believe this, but...I have a date on Friday."

"A date!" She clamps her hand over her mouth. "That's great, Raven."

I bite my lip. "I don't know if it's great. The lawyer's a nice guy, and pretty good-looking too." I look down. "Why he wants to go out with me though..."

She scoffs. "Are you kidding me? Why *wouldn't* he want to? You're beautiful."

"Um...I don't have hair, Savannah."

"Hair grows back, Ray."

I'm touched by her use of my nickname. I'm not sure she's done that before now.

"I guess I'm interested," I say. "I mean, like I said. He's very intelligent, good-looking, nice."

She rubs her thumb against her index and middle fingers. "And he's a lawyer."

I laugh. "That's probably more of a selling point for you than for me."

"Nothing's a selling point for me," Savannah says. "I'm madly in love with your brother. I've never met anyone like him. It's like..." She gazes out the kitchen window.

I raise a hand to stop her. "You don't have to finish that thought. I'm not sure I want to hear about how great my brother is in bed."

"Oh." Savannah blushes. "I wasn't going to go into any detail. I was just going to say that when you know, you know. The first time I laid eyes on your brother, I knew something was different about him. The attraction was immediate. Which of itself is not unusual, but it was just different with him. I can't really describe how."

"I think I understand."

She raises her eyebrows. "Do you?"

Damn it. I spoke without thinking. I got so comfortable talking to Savannah that I forgot we barely know each other.

I've almost let slip something juicy, and now she wants details.

But I can't go into detail.

Because those feelings? That ridiculous attraction that you think may be different from anything else you've ever felt?

I *have* had them.

The first time I laid eyes on Savannah's brother.

16

VINNIE

"I suppose it could be nothing," Falcon says. "Maybe there really *is* a reason for the EPA to be involved."

I scratch my chin. "I don't know. I haven't seen the property."

"Do you want to see the property?"

"Yeah, I probably should at some point. I'll be in touch when it's possible."

Grandfather expects to see me at the office early every morning, but I'll tell him I have an appointment. If he asks who with? I'll tell him it's none of his fucking business.

Weakness is not something my grandfather tolerates. Showing my strength, while it may annoy him and anger him, will ultimately lead to him respecting me.

"So what about the ladies?" I say. "Do we tell them what's going on? Or do we just let them think everything's taken care of?"

Falcon shakes his head, rubbing his hands over his stubbled cheeks. "I don't like keeping things from your sister. Or my sister. But damn, I wish Ray weren't even involved. She needs her strength. She needs to focus on healing. She's got this idea of starting this foundation. In fact, she met with an attorney yesterday and is getting things set up for it. I get that she needs something to focus on, take her mind off of the last several years. But what she really needs is to be resting."

I hold up a finger. "Actually, this foundation may be something good for her. It will help keep her mind off the rest of this. So while I agree with you that I don't like lying to either of them, I think let's keep it between us for now."

Falcon nods. "Agreed."

"Hey, you guys," Savannah yells down from up in the kitchen. "Dinner is served."

I finish the rest of my Scotch and soda and set the glass on the bar. I follow Falcon up the short stairway and into his and Savannah's giant gourmet kitchen, where Savannah has set four places at the solid oak kitchen table.

I noticed yesterday when I came over that they have a huge formal dining room across from the living room and off the foyer as you walk into the house.

Looks like it could seat about twenty people. It's similar to the dining room in my grandfather's house.

Fuck. Once he dies, that will be my house.

Ever since I returned to the States, I've wondered which will come first. My takedown of the family crime circuit from within, or my grandfather's natural demise.

It's more likely that my efforts will outlive him, and I'll still have my work cut out for me once he does die.

But the fucker's in remarkable health for a man over eighty. He could be around for another ten years. Hell, I wouldn't put it past him to round out a full century out of spite. I have seven years before Belinda McAllister comes of age. If I haven't taken down the family by then, I'll be forced to marry her.

"You sit here, Vinnie," Savannah says, gesturing to the seat across from Falcon.

On my right side is Savannah, and on my left, Raven.

And it's hard not to stare at her. She's so damned beautiful. Those dark eyes, I swear to God, could see inside a person's soul.

I feel like if I let her look at me, she'll see all my secrets. Everything that happened to me. So much I don't want her to know.

Sure, the worst thing that has ever happened to me occurred back in Long Island, in my grandfather's study.

But Europe wasn't exactly an oasis.

Once we're seated, Savannah passes around the salad bowl and a plate of garlic bread. The lasagna sits in the center of the table. It smells wonderful, and the aroma takes me back not to my time in Italy, but to my childhood. When Serafina made the best lasagna ever.

Savannah and Raven are both beaming.

They think everything has been taken care of.

I hope to God they're right.

"Vinnie," Savannah says, "Falcon and I can't thank you enough for taking care of this."

I lift my eyebrows at Falcon, and he nods slightly at me. "I'd do anything for you, Sav. I only wish I'd been here to save you from what you went through."

"We've been over and over that," she says. "You did what you felt you had to do."

I close my eyes then, thinking about my younger brother. About how he might still be alive if I hadn't left.

"Let it go, Vinnie," Savannah says. "Mikey's in a better place now."

"I suppose." I take a bite of bread. The garlic and buttery goodness slide across my tongue.

"Raven made the garlic bread," Savannah says.

I swallow. "Did you? It's delicious." I smile at Raven.

A luscious pink pops up on her cheeks. "I'm glad you like it."

"It's great. How did you make it?"

"Well..." A playful grin spreads across her gorgeous face. "I mixed some garlic with butter, spread it on some bread, and put it in the oven."

Savannah laughs. "Well, it is delicious, Ray."

Yeah, I'm an idiot. Everybody knows how to make garlic bread. It *is* delicious though. All garlic bread is.

But this garlic bread, crafted by this beautiful woman, takes the cake. My face warms as I grab another piece, hoping Raven doesn't see how red I'm getting.

What makes me act like a stupid schoolboy around this woman?

Damn, I've got it bad.

I don't say much more as I finish my bread and salad. Then Savannah serves each of us a huge chunk of lasagna.

I take a bite, and it's delicious. Not quite as good as I remember from my childhood, but every bit as good as anything I ate in Italy.

"Sav, it's wonderful."

She beams from across the table. "Glad you like it, Vinnie."

Raven gushes then, "Oh my God, I think this is the best lasagna I've ever tasted. It's elegant."

Savannah laughs at that. "*Elegant?* Now I know you're pulling my leg, Raven."

"Well, since the last lasagna I had was hospital food..." She shrugs. "And like I told you. Everything tastes better now. It's like my tastebuds have exploded or something."

I smile at her then. She's so vibrant and full of life. She's looked her life in the eye and come out on the other end ready to live the hell out of it. I'm filled with the need to get to know this woman. To find out what makes her tick. And my God—those full pink lips.

What might they feel like against my own?

For a moment, I imagine her naked. Her body devoid of all hair. Only her pink pussy visible.

"Vinnie?" Savannah says.

I snap out of my daydream. "Yeah?"

She chuckles lightly. "You've been holding that piece of lasagna on your fork halfway to your mouth for like a minute now."

I quickly bring it to my mouth, chew, and swallow. "Just thinking."

"I know." Savannah pats my hand from across the table. "You're back now, back in a life you never wanted. I'm sorry for that, Vinnie."

I'll let her think that's what I was thinking about. I suppose she isn't wrong. I have a lot on my plate, and I'm not talking lasagna.

"So Falcon," Savannah says, "did Raven tell you she has a date Friday?"

That bite of lasagna I swallowed turns into a cannonball in my stomach.

Raven has a date?

"I don't ever like to think about my sisters having dates," Falcon says. "But that's great, Raven. Who are you seeing?"

Raven swallows the bite of lasagna in her mouth. "This lawyer who helped me today. His name is Brick Latham."

I nearly choke on the sip of wine I just drank. "Brick?"

"Yeah, that's his name."

"I suppose he has a brother named Stone and a sister named Marble?" My tone is more pointed than I intend.

"Uh…" Falcon clears his throat. "Our grandfather's name was Brick. Brick Bellamy."

I put my fork down, avoiding eye contact with Raven in the process. God damn it. Now I feel like an asshole. I shouldn't have made fun of the name in the first place. I didn't mean anything by it. I was taken aback that Raven has a date.

Why shouldn't she have a date? If I see how beautiful she is, why wouldn't another man? She doesn't need hair to be beautiful.

And her hair will grow back. It's already growing back. She's got a raven-black buzz cut now, and damn…

"I'm sorry." I wipe my lips on my napkin. "I don't know what just got into me. It's not like Vincent is the greatest name in the world. Or Vinnie."

"It's Daddy's name," Savannah says. "But I like the name Brick. It sounds strong."

"The name Vincent is associated with strength and victory," I say. "It's derived from Latin, meaning to conquer."

And why the fuck did I just say that? To my sister of all people?

Raven looks at me, and damn, those eyes… They pierce me.

And as she looks at me, I can't tell if she's angry or ready to burst out laughing.

Either reaction would be warranted. I'm being a dick.

I had my fair share of women while I was overseas. I never got serious with anyone, but I had a lot of sex with a lot of hot babes.

Now, for the first time in a long time, I've met a woman I actually like. A woman I'd like to get to know. A woman I'm extremely attracted to.

And what do I do?

I make fun of the name of her date. A name that her grandfather shares.

God, I'm back in high school...

What a fuck-up.

Raven takes a sip of her water. "I think Vincent is a lovely name."

I widen my eyes at Raven. Did she really just say that?

"So is Raven," I say. "It's a beautiful name, and it fits you."

She smiles at me then. Raven Bellamy smiles at me. So I clear my throat. "I apologize. I shouldn't have made fun of your date's name. Your grandfather's name, though I didn't know he shared it."

"You don't need to apologize. You were making a joke." She smiles again. "Jokes are funny. Jokes make people laugh. People don't laugh enough." She wrinkles her nose like an adorable little bunny. "When you look death in the face, all you want to do is go back to a time in life when you were laughing. When life was good, and you were happy."

I stop my jaw from dropping.

I hardly know this woman. But in that moment, I fall a little bit in love with Raven Bellamy.

17

RAVEN

I love the feeling of being full.

I finished my entire square of lasagna.

It was a big heavy square.

For so long, I had no appetite. I didn't want to eat, and when I did eat, I ate disgusting hospital food. Half the time it didn't even stay down.

Since I've been feeling better, I've learned to enjoy the taste of food again. The feeling of having a full tummy.

It's been wonderful.

Vinnie and Falcon are talking across the table about some bourbon that Vinnie wants Falcon to try.

I of course can't drink. While the rest of them are enjoying a bottle of Chianti, my wine glass is filled with water.

That's fine. I was never a big drinker anyway. But I did enjoy wine.

That was something Falcon and I had in common. He and Mom were supposed to go on this big wine tour the year after he graduated from college.

That didn't happen, of course. It didn't happen because Falcon went to prison.

Mom canceled the wine tour, but the next summer, she asked me to accompany her.

I loved it. I had never been quite as much of oenophile as Falcon was, but after that wine tour in France and Italy, I learned to love the elixir of grapes as much as my mother and Falcon did. I always felt bad that he missed that special trip with Mom. Robin had no interest in going to wine country. She went to Barbados with a group of college friends instead.

When there's a lull in the conversation, I turn to Vinnie. "Do you like wine, Vinnie?"

He raises his eyebrows at me.

"I mean, I see your glass is empty."

"Oh, Vinnie, I'm sorry." Savannah grabs the wine bottle. "Did you want some more?"

"No," he says. "I'm fine. I had two drinks with Falcon before dinner, and I have to drive home." Then he turns to me. "But to answer your question, yes. I like wine. When I was in Europe, I drank a lot of wine. Especially in France and Italy. Some Spanish wines were really great too. But what really surprised me were the Portuguese wines. Some of them were quite good."

I nod, trying to mask my admiration for Vinnie's worldliness. "I used to love wine. I toured French and Italian wine country with my mother the summer after I finished college. It's something I miss."

"You'll be able to drink again soon," Savannah says. "Right?"

"Yeah. Once I'm off these higher dosages of medication. I should be able to have a glass or two."

"Do you like Italian wine?" Vinnie asks.

"Yeah. I think I like it better than French wine, which I know is heresy."

Vinnie smiles at me, and I feel a pulse between my legs.

"I do too," he agrees.

"So do I," Falcon says.

"Tell me about the Chianti," I say to Vinnie. "Tell me what I'm missing."

Savannah examines the label of the bottle. "This is just a regular Chianti I found in the liquor store in downtown Summer Creek. It's nothing special."

"But it was perfect with this lasagna," Vinnie says. "You don't always need to have the best wine. Sometimes an easily drinkable wine can perfectly complement the meal you're serving." He leans toward me, smiling gently. "I think you would've liked it, Raven. It was acidic, so it went great with the tomato sauce. And it had basic Chianti notes of fresh berries and red fruit. It was delicious."

I close my eyes, imagining the wine floating over my tongue. "It sounds amazing." When I open my eyes again, all three of them are staring at me. "What?"

"You just look so peaceful," Falcon says. "It's good to see, Ray."

I sigh. "I just appreciate everything so much more now. Not that I would wish this on any of you guys, but I almost feel like I've been given a gift. The sky is bluer, the grass is greener. And the thought of Chianti flowing over my tongue is that much more exciting. It will be wonderful when I can finally take a drink of it myself."

"How long will that be?" Vinnie asks.

"If I continue to do well, the doctors will wean me off my medication."

"And you *will* continue to do well," Falcon says.

"I will," I assert.

One thing I learned during cancer treatment is that attitude is everything. There were times it wasn't possible to stay as positive as I would've liked, but I did my best. I never thought of myself as sick or dying.

And now I'm not.

I'm alive. Thanks to my brother for the most part. But I like to think my willingness to fight helped quite a bit, too. The bone marrow transplant was not guaranteed to work.

"Did anyone save room for dessert?" Savannah asks.

I give her a smile. "Yes. Never again will I forgo dessert. I want to appreciate the small things in life. And if it means I weigh a few more pounds than I did before I got sick, so be it."

"I love that attitude," Savannah says. "But dessert isn't much. It's just vanilla bean ice cream with raspberries."

I close my eyes, imagining the creamy vanilla and the sweetness of the raspberries. "It sounds perfect."

"How about you, Vinnie?" Savannah asks. "You want dessert?"

"I should pass," he says. "I need to get back. It's a long drive to Austin."

"I understand," Savannah says. "But you need to come by more often, Vinnie. I don't want to miss any more of my big brother than I already have."

"You know what then?" Vinnie flashes a smile—God, he's so damned good-looking—at Savannah. "I will have dessert.

It's not like I'm watching my weight. What's a couple more minutes?"

Savannah smiles at him. "That's great, Vinnie."

"You need help?" I ask.

"Nope. Just sit down. I'll have it over to all of you guys in a jiffy."

A moment later, Savannah slides a dish with two scoops of vanilla bean ice cream dotted with fresh raspberries in front of me.

I don't wait until someone else starts. Once everyone is served, I take a spoonful of the ice cream along with a raspberry and slide it between my lips.

The vanilla, the cream, the sweet tanginess of the raspberry. It's all so perfect and wonderful.

When I open my eyes, Vinnie is staring at me. I widen my eyes at him.

"I'm sorry. It's just... Watching you eat is really mesmerizing."

I blink a few times. "Oh?"

Vinnie presses his lips together as a small rush of pinkness hits his cheeks. "I mean... Yeah. The way I said it sounds weird. But what I mean is it's fascinating watching you appreciate every bite. Taking the time to savor something as simple as vanilla ice cream with some berries. I think the world could learn a lot from you, Raven."

A cozy warmth envelops my entire body, especially my face. "I'm no different from anyone else who's survived this horrible disease. I'm one of the lucky ones, honestly. A lot of people don't make it." I swallow back a rush of emotion as it hits my core. "And I'm just...so *thankful*."

"You're really something," he says.

His words make my cheeks heat further. Make my tummy flutter. I'm surprised the heat from my body isn't melting the ice cream in front of me. Vinnie makes that place between my legs—that place I haven't let myself think about in so long—want something.

Something I never thought I'd want again.

I always had a healthy sex drive. But then the treatment—the chemo especially—made my libido wane significantly. That coupled with the sheer exhaustion of trying to stay alive while my sickness ravaged my body rendered me numb to any sort of sexual feeling for the longest time.

"Thank you," I say. "I guess."

"To be fair," Falcon says, "this is really good ice cream."

That gets a laugh out of everyone at the table.

I take another bite, shyly looking away from Vinnie.

Still I feel his gaze on me. It's hot and raw.

And I wonder if he feels the same thing I do.

Probably not. I'm bald. And still recovering from cancer.

But for a moment I wish things were different.

And I wish I hadn't accepted that date with Brick Latham.

But the chances of someone as good-looking as Vinnie looking my way?

They're not good.

We finish our ice cream, and all four of us take our dishes over to the counter.

"You need any help?" Vinnie asks.

And I like him even more.

Savannah raises an eyebrow. "Wow, you *did* change over in Europe." She lets out a humorless chuckle. "No man in our family would ever think of asking if he could help clean up the dishes."

"Our family is going to change, Sav." Vinnie stacks a few plates and gathers some silverware off the table. "You can bet your life on that."

"Well, I appreciate you asking, but I've got this covered." Savannah takes the stack of plates and starts rinsing them off in the sink. "Go on downstairs and relax."

"Actually," I say, "I should be getting home. If you don't mind, Falcon."

"Of course not, Ray."

"I could take you," Vinnie says.

My cheeks warm once more.

He scratches the side of his head. "I mean, I'm going anyway. Like I said, I have to get moving. It's a long drive to Austin."

"I would take you a little out of your way," I say. "Mom and Dad's place is on the other side of the ranch."

"I don't mind. And it will save you a trip, Falcon. Since I'm leaving anyway."

The thought of being alone in a car with Vinnie scares me.

And not in a bad way.

18

VINNIE

Raven doesn't talk much during the ride. But the quiet doesn't seem to bother her. The look on her face is so serene. Like she's happy. Happy in a way that perhaps she's never been before.

I ache to reach out and touch her.

But I've got so much going on, and she's fragile right now. Perhaps not mentally fragile but physically.

And I'm betrothed to an eleven-year-old girl...

God, the thought of it makes me sick to my stomach.

Raven gives me directions through the private roads on the Bellamy property to get to her parents' large ranch house.

And boy, is it large—a sprawling Spanish-inspired masterpiece.

I drive up the brick driveway.

"Thank you for the ride," she says. "I realize you went out of your way, and I appreciate it."

"It wasn't that far out of my way. I have a long drive anyway."

She reaches for the door handle, but I stop her. "Just a second."

I get out of the driver-side door and walk around to open the passenger door. I give her my hand, and she takes it delicately.

When she stands next to me, she's so close I can actually feel her breath on my neck.

"I'll see you to the door."

She looks away shyly. "You don't have to."

"I know I don't have to, Raven." I give her hand a light squeeze. "I'm trying to be a gentleman here."

"Well... All right."

Beneath the security lights from her home, I can see her cheeks blush. A gorgeous rosy tint.

Nubs of black lashes are growing on her eyelids, and her eyebrows, which she's penciled in lightly, are also starting to grow.

My God, she's so beautiful.

I offer my arm to her and she takes it. And when she stumbles a bit, I steady her.

"You okay?"

"Yes." She closes her eyes for a moment. "Some of my meds make me lightheaded sometimes."

Bummer. I was hoping *I* was the one who made her lightheaded.

I swallow. "Raven..."

"Yes?"

I open my mouth to say something, but before I can, something takes me over. I pull her to me, not gently at all. Then I kiss her.

Her lips are already parted, and I dive right in.

A soft moan vibrates from her throat and into me, spurring me on.

I've kissed a lot of women in my lifetime. Even a man once—in Italy—but no kiss has ever been as wonderful and amazing as this one.

Her tongue is soft, and she tastes of the vanilla and raspberries of our dessert. To my surprise, she kisses me back.

All I can think about is what her beautiful body might look like naked. Splayed out on the bed as a feast for me. Not just for my body, but for all five of my senses. My eyes, ears, nose.

I inhale her sweet scent. Raspberries again. Plus something woodsy. Maybe a touch of caramel.

I kiss her and I kiss her and I kiss her…

Until I realize what I'm doing and I break the kiss.

Her lips are darker and more swollen than they were at dinner. I kissed her hard. And I'd do it again.

Her hand absently wanders to her lower lip.

"I shouldn't have done that," I say.

"I'm not complaining," she says softly.

"Do you have any idea how beautiful you are?"

More blush on those gorgeous cheeks. She says nothing.

"I've never seen a woman as beautiful as you."

"I look a lot like my sister. I mean, we're not identical twins, but…" She frowns. "Plus she has hair."

I can no longer resist the urge to touch her. I slide my hand over her head, letting the short growth of hair tickle my fingers. She winces a bit.

"Please," I say. "Don't. This is you right now. You're beautiful. You couldn't possibly be any more beautiful with a gorgeous mane of hair."

"Actually, I could," she says, her voice shaking. "You've seen Falcon's hair. Mine is even longer and thicker. Well, thicker. It will be a while before it's longer."

I move my hand from her head and tip her chin up so that she meets my gaze. "I shouldn't have kissed you, Raven. There are a million reasons why I shouldn't have. But I can't bring myself to be sorry about it."

"I don't recall asking you to." She breaks her gaze from mine. "But you should know..."

"Know what?"

"I... I don't know. Perhaps I'm being presumptuous, but I have a date Friday night."

I take a step backward. "You mentioned that at dinner, remember?"

"Oh. Right." She blushes darker red. "My meds... I forget sometimes. I shouldn't be so presumptuous anyway. Just because you kissed me doesn't mean..."

Doesn't mean what? That I want to take her on a date?

She's right. I don't want to take her out. I want to take her straight to my bed. I can't have a relationship with her. I'm promised to someone else, at least for now. Plus, how can I drag her into the mess that is my family right now? I'm determined to take down my grandfather and all of his minions. I may not be able to get my father out of prison, but I can at least take down the people who helped put him there.

"Break the date," I tell her.

I hear the tone of my voice. I hear the command. I have no right to make this demand of her, but I do it anyway. It just kind of pops out.

"I'm not sure I can," she says. "You see, he's the attorney

who's helping me with my nonprofit. And if I break the date..."

"Break it," I command again.

"I..."

"Look. You have an excuse built right in. You shouldn't be dating him because you're working together on your nonprofit." I look her straight into her beautiful brown eyes. "Break it," I say through gritted teeth.

Her lips part, and she lets out a tiny gasp.

I slide my hand over the apple of her cheek. God, her skin is like silk. "I'm not kidding, Raven. Break that date."

"I don't know..." She draws in a breath. "What do you want from me, Vinnie?"

I lean in and growl into her ear, "I want everything. I want to kiss those lips until they bleed, Raven."

She gasps again at those words.

Frankly, I'm not even sure where they came from.

How can I want a woman this much? I had plenty of sex overseas. More than most men have during their whole lives. My share of women and even one man. I've had threesomes and foursomes. I've had lovemaking sessions that lasted days.

I was only celibate during my time at the Buddhist temple.

The rest of the time?

If I had an offer of sex, I took it. And I had a lot of offers. European women loved me.

But now?

All I want is *this* woman. This woman who I should leave alone. Who I shouldn't drag into my life.

My grandfather told me to end the life of this beautiful woman.

I refused, of course. Who could even think of such evil? Of taking this glorious life away from the world?

But that's what I'm dealing with. Evil. Pure evil.

And I can't drag Raven into any of that.

So I'm going to walk away.

I'm going to walk to my car and drive away.

I take a step to do so, but Raven grabs me, pulls me into her embrace, threads her fingers through my hair, and brings her lips to mine.

19

RAVEN

It's been years since I've kissed a man.

Years since I've wanted to.

When you're sick, the last thing on your mind is kissing and sex. All you can think about is getting better, and you're willing to give up anything—and I mean *anything*—to make it happen.

You make deals with God. With whatever higher power you believe in. You make promises. Promises you'll never be able to keep.

You leverage everything you can, anything in the world to get better.

To not leave this earth.

To not die.

And now I'm kissing this man.

The most gorgeous man I've ever laid eyes on. A man who could have any woman. Women with hair.

My hair will grow back. It's already well on its way. This morning I saw the beginnings of my eyelashes and eyebrows in the mirror.

I'll even be happy to see my pubic hair.

All those hairs I used to pluck out, shave, trim—everything I hated, everything that made me feel like the link between man and the ape.

Now I look at that hair in a totally different way.

Vinnie's lips are so soft, yet they kiss me with a hardness I'm not sure I've ever experienced. But not hardness in a bad way. In his kiss, I feel how he wants me. How he's attracted to me.

And it's crazy, you know? Crazy that he would want me.

But he does.

And I love the feeling. I love the feeling of being beautiful again. I may not be beautiful to myself when I look in the mirror, but I'm beautiful to Vinnie. Why would he be kissing me otherwise?

He slides his tongue farther into my mouth, and my God, he has a big tongue. I swear he's searching every corner of my mouth, and I'm loving every minute of it. I twirl my tongue with his, desperately seeking something.

Something...

And I know what it is.

I know what it is because my nipples are hard. My pussy is throbbing. My legs are weak, my knees unsteady.

I remember this feeling.

And damn...

I was ready to give everything up so I could live.

But who can live without this feeling? This incredible feeling of the meeting of two hearts and souls?

Or at least of two bodies.

I'm not sure his heart is involved, even if mine may be.

The kiss lingers, and my God, I don't want it to end. I want it only to go on. I want it to lead to the inevitable. Vinnie sliding his lips over every part of my body, Vinnie's cock inside me.

I slide my fingers over his broad shoulders, down his sides, over his hips, and then to the front of him, where I—

He jerks backward.

"We can't go there," he says.

My hand is still on his crotch. On the giant bulge that proves how much he wants me.

"I understand," I say.

He looks at me, blinking. "I'm not sure you do." He closes his eyes. "It's not that I don't want to, Raven. Your beauty is... It had to be carved in the heavens. No one on earth could create something like you."

I stand there, my mouth agape. I don't know what to say to him. I'm bald. Hairless. Still kind of skinny.

But he sees something.

Easy to see what I see in him. He's a god. Dark hair, dark eyes. His Italian blood is so much more evident than Savannah's is. He's a gorgeous Mediterranean Italian man.

Hair even thicker than my brothers'.

"In another world," he continues. "Another time, another place... I'd love to explore something with you."

"I know about your engagement," I say. "I don't care, Vinnie."

He shakes his head and takes a step back. "That's not even what I'm talking about. I don't plan to marry that girl. I've got seven years before she comes of age, and she's not going to want to be married to a man over forty at that point."

Vinnie's already so good-looking. In his forties? When a little more silver starts to show at his temples and he has some more crinkly laugh lines around his eyes? His stubble turns to salt-and-pepper?

He'll be even more good-looking.

"But you told me to break my date," I say.

He frowns. "I did. I shouldn't have."

"The tone of your voice. It was… It made me want to obey you. Made me want to break the date."

"I had no right to say that to you."

"But you did, Vinnie. Why?"

He takes another step back and rubs at his lips. "Because, damn it. Don't you see? There's something about you, Raven. Something is pulling me toward you. And I should never have indulged myself. Never should've kissed you."

I take a step forward, cocking my head. "So you regret it?"

"God no."

"Then what is it, Vinnie?" I place a hand on his chest. "I'm not asking you for anything. You're the one asking me for something. You're asking me to break my date."

"Raven, if you want to go out with that lawyer, then go out with him." He draws in a deep breath.

I bite my lip. "I don't want to. What if I tell you I'd like to go out with you instead?"

"Then I'd be the happiest man on earth." He looks down. "And also the worst man on earth."

I grab his hands. "You're not your family, Vinnie. I know that. Falcon and Savannah know that."

"Damn it, Raven." He whips his hands out of mine. "You shouldn't even be involved in this."

"I'm sure my brothers agree with you. But I *am* involved. I'm not some weak little woman who has to be protected."

"None of us think that."

I can't resist rolling my eyes. "Don't you? You're thinking it now."

"I'm not," he says. "I just... You've already been through the wringer." He gazes deep into my eyes. "I couldn't bear it if something ever happened to you."

A chill runs down my back. "You want me. I can't believe it, but you seem to."

"How could you not believe it?"

I don't answer him. Instead I run my hand over my head.

He steps toward me, caressing my cheek. "You're much more than any head of hair, Raven. Your beauty shines from within. Sure, you have fine features—a classic beauty by anyone's standards." He drops his hands and wraps them around my waist. "There's something more. Something underneath that makes you glow. Maybe it's your new lease on life. Or maybe it's just *you*, Raven. All I know is I've never seen anything like it. Never felt what I'm feeling right now."

I take a step back, my mouth agape. I can't believe a man as attractive as Vinnie just said those things to me. Me, a woman in recovery from a deadly disease, who is starting to look better but still has a long way to go.

"I'm truly beautiful to you?" I ask.

"God, yes." He moves forward and cups both my cheeks. Stares straight into my eyes. "You're the most beautiful thing I've ever laid eyes on. I thought so the first time I saw you. I even mentioned it to Falcon and Savannah."

"You haven't seen my sister yet," I tell him.

He chuckles. "You think that matters? I'm sure your sister is beautiful. I'm sure your mother's beautiful. I mean, she'd have to be to produce you. But I'm not just talking about your outer beauty. Surely you know that."

"You don't even know me." I look down. "How do you know what I'm like on the inside?"

He tips my chin up. "I can't explain it. Just something I felt the first time I laid eyes on you. The feeling has only grown as I've gotten to know you. When you asked me to describe the wine tonight. When I watched you eat a bite of ice cream." He cracks a small, sweet smile. "You're just so...perfect." His smile vanishes and he looks away. "Which is why you don't belong in my life."

I draw in a deep breath. "First, I'm not perfect."

"I don't mean *perfect* perfect." He rakes his hands through his hair. "I don't know how to explain it. I don't think there's a word in the English language. I know you're not perfect. I know you aren't infallible. No one is. But to me... When I look at you... It's like I see the person I've never even allowed myself to dream about."

Oh my God...

If he weren't holding me, I think I might swoon.

For someone who claims he can't find the word in the English language, he certainly knows how to use all the others.

I touch his stubbled cheek, scrape my fingernails over it. "I'll break the date."

He widens his eyes, but then his lips turn downward. "I can't offer you anything. I'm not in any position to."

"Did I ask you for anything?"

"No, but this lawyer fellow. He might be looking for a relationship. He might be able to give you things that I can't."

"Vinnie," I say, "I'm not asking for anything except for today. For this moment. How could I ask for anything else? For years, I wasn't sure I'd even *have* a future." I gaze up at the night sky, take in every shining star. “I have one now, and I’m determined to enjoy every single second of it. If that means not looking past tomorrow, so be it.” I return my gaze to his. “Right now, that kiss you gave me… It was unlike anything I’ve ever experienced, and while it has been a while, I have kissed a lot of men. So in this moment? My only desire is to kiss you again.”

He groans. A groan that sounds almost like a growl.

Then he pulls me to him and crushes his mouth to mine.

20

VINNIE

I may burn in hell for this, but at the moment I don't care.

I need her. I want her. And I'm going to take her.

Falcon will probably kill me, but it would be a sweet death.

I devour her mouth. I let my hand slide up her belly to her chest, where I cup her breasts.

The perfect size, more than a handful, and I can feel her hard nipples through her bra and blouse.

She gasps into my throat as I give her nipple a pinch.

I break the kiss quickly. "Where? Where can I take you?"

"I… I have my own home. I've just been staying at Mom and Dad's. You know, while I recover…"

She has her own home.

I don't. Not yet. I'm staying at my parents' house, helping Mom get used to not having Dad there.

"Are you sure?"

She nods. "I don't think I've ever been more sure of anything."

"Your house far from here?"

"About ten minutes."

I open the door for her, and she slides back into the passenger seat.

I get in the driver seat, but before I start the car I turn to her. "Are you sure? Because if you're not, tell me now. And I'll understand. If your body is too weak, if you don't think you can do this—"

"Stop it," she says, her tone slightly acidic. "Just stop it now, Vinnie. Do not treat me like I'm some weakling. You want to hear what I want? I want you to fuck me. I want you to fuck me so hard that I don't know where I am. Even *who* I am." She grabs my hand and squeezes it. "It's been so long, Vinnie. I never thought I'd have these feelings again. I never thought I'd *want* these feelings again. And frankly? What I'm feeling right now is so much different from anything I've ever felt. So much better. So much more... I yearn for you. I ache for you."

My blood is boiling. "Raven, God."

"I want you to use me up," she says. "Use my body. Take me until there's nothing else."

I suck in a breath.

"I feel like an animal," she continues. "That's how intense this urge is."

I adjust my groin. "Yeah, I know exactly what you mean."

"Then take me to my home."

"Will your parents worry?"

"I can text them. Tell them I'm spending the night with Falcon and Savannah. That way they won't worry."

Damn, she's thought of everything.

"Do you have everything you need? I mean, I don't want you to be without —"

She places two fingers over my mouth to stop me from talking. "I have everything I need in my purse. I always come prepared. So please, Vinnie. Please just take me home."

My body is on fire as I start the engine of my car.

This is happening.

And damn...

I know I'm going to hell.

This is a woman who deserves everything. She deserves a man who can fall in love with her. Give her a family, children.

Not a man who's got "kill Giacomo Puzo" on his to-do list.

But I can't stop now.

Just for tonight, I will allow myself this release. To be with a woman who is an angel in every sense of the word.

Raven directs me to her home.

It's a ranch house, smaller than her parents', but about the same size as Falcon and Savannah's.

Which is still pretty damn huge. These people have money that I can't even conceive of. And growing up in a mob family, we always had a lot of money. But nothing like this.

Raven's house stretches out across the landscape, clad in a beautiful mix of natural stone and dark wood with a gently sloped roof covered in slate tiles. The front entrance is framed by large floor-to-ceiling windows with black iron frames.

I pull into the driveway, but she doesn't wait for me to help her out of her side of the door this time.

She gets out quickly, and I meet her on her side of the car. A wide covered porch wraps around the front and back of the mansion, and several wooden patio chairs and a suspended wooden bench furnish the area.

We walk briskly to her solid oak front door, which bears some impressive carvings of Texas bluebonnets. Raven keys in a code and opens it.

Her house is magnificent. The high ceilings of its foyer, adorned with rustic wooden beams, draw my eyes upward to a large wrought-iron chandelier. I don't notice much more before I grab her and kiss her again.

And this time it's a kiss of promise.

Not a promise for the future, of course, but a promise for the night to come.

Her words echo in my head.

I want you to fuck me. I want you to fuck me so hard that I don't know where I am. Even who *I am.*

That's what I want too.

I want to forget who I am. I want to forget that I'm Vincent Gallo, Junior, heir to the Bianchi crime family.

I want to forget what's in front of me, what I'll be forced to do.

Who I'll be forced to kill.

I break the kiss, and rasp out, "Bedroom?"

She takes my hand, leads me through the foyer and down a hallway to the end where she opens the door to a huge master suite.

The room is bathed in moonlight from the large windows, the silver rays casting a mystical glow over every surface. Some would call it romantic. The scent of her perfume fills the room, intoxicating and enticing. Her king-sized canopy bed is neatly made, but by the end of the night, I know it won't be.

Raven pulls me toward her, her lips finding mine in another searing kiss. She tastes of temptation, sweet and all-consuming. I explore her body, tracing the curves that have been teasing my imagination.

Our movements are urgent as if we're racing against time —which we are, in ways she doesn't know. We're fused together at our mouths, both moaning and groaning. Though we're still fully clothed, I can feel her heart stampeding against her chest like a wild horse. Every gasp she lets out fuels my desire even more.

She clings to the lapels of my jacket and pushes it over my shoulders. Her every touch is like an electrical current that ignites me from within. I deepen the kiss—a desperate kiss that echoes the turmoil of emotions rioting inside me.

Her moans are like sweet music to my ears, spurring me on. With each gasp and shiver that courses through her body against mine, my last vestiges of control slip away. A beautiful surrender it is—her to me, me to her—giving in to the unspoken promise of pleasure that this night holds.

She digs her nails into my back, pulling me closer and closer until there's no space left between us. We're entwined with each other in such a way that it's hard to tell where one person ends and the other begins.

"Vinnie," she whispers between gasps, breaking the kiss. The way she says my name sends shivers running down my spine. She's summoning me, drawing me in deeper, urging me to lose myself completely.

"Yes," I breathe into her ear, unable to form any coherent words beyond that. And why should I? Words have no place here. Actions speak louder than any phrase ever could.

I gaze into her eyes and I see more than lust.

I can't look away, even though I know I should. I see a promise of something more, maybe even something akin to love. But it scares me more than anything else. Love is dangerous, lethal in its own way. Love brings vulnerability, and vulnerability is not something I can afford right now.

So I won't fall in love with this woman.

I can't.

I shouldn't even be doing what we're doing.

But it's too late for me to stop now. I can't stop. I don't want to.

She asked me to take her. To use her up. That I can do. Guilt will creep in tomorrow, but I'll deal with it then.

She's wearing a simple T-shirt and baggy blue jeans. Nothing fancy, but on her they're sexier than the skimpiest lingerie.

My jacket is on the floor, but I'm still in my shirt, trousers, and tie, and right now the necktie seems to be choking me.

I loosen it, and she puts her hands over mine.

"Let me."

With her long and delicate fingers, she slackens and removes it, setting it neatly on a bed table.

Then she unbuttons my first button, her fingers grazing against my flesh.

If possible, my cock grows even harder.

Everything about Raven Bellamy is so delicate. To touch her might shatter that delicacy, but I've already touched her, already kissed her. Already flicked one of those delicious nipples between my thumb and forefinger. I can't wait to do it when nothing separates us. When I can see her beauty unencumbered by clothes.

But apparently she's going to undress me first.

I'm not used to that. I like to get a woman naked. Perhaps it's a control thing, but I like to see a woman in her nude and vulnerable state before I present myself.

With Raven? If this is how she wants to proceed, I'm all in. It scares me how much I want to give this woman everything. Even when it goes against my nature.

I'm *not* a gentle soul.

I never was, but after my grandfather molested me on my eighteenth birthday, any remaining gentleness got thrown out of me.

I don't make love gently either.

Raven, though she looks so delicate and porcelain and perfect, asked me to use her. Use her up.

Fuck, does she even know what those words did to me?

Does she know what I'm capable of?

I spent seventeen years in Europe, and during that time I did a lot of soul-searching. But my ultimate conclusion was that I am a product of my upbringing. Some things about me I can never change. I had to make peace with that.

I had to come home, take my place. I had to do it for Savannah. For the memory of Mikey.

She finishes unbuttoning my shirt, slides it over my shoulders, and lays it gently next to my necktie.

And I'm done with gentle.

I want to see clothes strewn on the floor. I want to see bodies entangled on the bed.

"Stop," I say on a growl.

She widens her beautiful eyes. "Am I doing something wrong?"

"Raven, I'm not sure you *could* do anything wrong."

"That's not true."

"That's not what I mean. You told me to use you. Use your body. So we're done with gentle here."

Her lips part, tremble just a touch. She stops it quickly, but I notice.

"So I'll ask you again. Is this what you want? Because after this, I'm done asking. I will take from you. And I won't stop."

She nibbles on her lower lip for a split second before nodding and kicking off her shoes. "I'm sure, Vinnie. I'm so very sure."

I grab her then, pull her to me, and press my lips to hers, shoving my tongue between them.

Another raw and ferocious kiss, and all that makes my cock throb harder.

I'm good with taking it slow. I'm going to savor every minute. I'll undress Raven slowly, even though I want to rip her clothes off her.

Slow is fine. But I'm done with gentle.

I glide my hands under her shirt and pull it up, revealing inch by inch of her perfect skin. She trembles beneath my touch. Or maybe I'm the one who's shaking. Either way, this is real and raw.

After I've stripped off her shirt, I toss it to the floor. Her chest rises and falls with each breath she takes.

I hook my fingers into the waistband of her jeans and meet her gaze. Her dark eyes are wide and full of fire. The intensity there sends a jolt straight to my gut. Damn, she has power. Raven has power she doesn't even know about. She could bring me down in a minute, and I'd go willingly.

I pull down her jeans, and they join her shirt on the floor.

She stands before me now in only a bra and panties, both lacy and white—innocent and provocative at the same time.

"Vinnie," she whispers.

My name in her voice is like a spell binding me to her. It's a plea, a confession, a prayer. It's all of those and none at the same time.

"Raven," I growl back, my voice heavy with longing. I find the clasp of her bra and snap it open. It joins the rest of her clothes on the floor.

Now she's standing in front of me only in her panties, her plump breasts falling gently against her chest. She's breathtaking, undeniably beautiful, but it's not just her physical beauty that draws me in. There's a strength about her in the way she carries herself. As if the storm of her illness made her stronger.

I lean down to kiss her just below her collarbone, trail my lips across her skin before I reach behind her and tug at the elastic waistband of her panties.

With a harsh grasp, I rip them from her.

She gasps.

Yeah, I'm so done being gentle.

"Vinnie...wait," she breathes.

"No," I growl, my heart pounding a primal beat in my chest. "No more waiting."

I pull her into my arms, crushing her soft curves against my hard planes. She wraps her arms around my neck as if she's holding on for dear life.

Is she?

With a swift and sudden movement, I sweep her off her feet and stride toward the bed. Her gasp echoes through the room.

As I lay her down on the silk sheets, her gaze never leaves mine. Her eyes are wide, filled with trust and a vulnerable desire that takes me to the edge.

I capture her lips in a searing kiss that leaves us both gasping for breath.

I linger there for a while, lost in the taste of her, until she pulls away just enough to look up at me. Her eyes are bright, full of expectancy and uncertainty.

"Vinnie," she whispers. "I want this. I want *you*."

The words hang heavy in the room, echoing in my mind as I search her eyes. Her vulnerability is clear, but so is her resolve. It's a potent mix that drives me even further into madness.

With a growl, I roam my hands down her body, tracing every curve and contour, trying to engrave them into my memory. Her skin is soft and warm under my touch.

Every gasp and moan from her lips sends jolts of pleasure through me. She wriggles beneath me as I edge my fingers closer to her core. When I reach the ultimate destination, I slide my fingers through her soft folds.

She's molten hot and ready for me.

Her breath hitches, a silent plea that I don't ignore. My fingers wet from her juices, I glide them over her clit. Her back arches up, pressing her chest against mine.

"Vinnie!"

"You're mine," I growl into her ear, my voice laced with possessiveness.

Even though I know I can't let myself fall for her, I'll die before anyone else touches her. She's mine to protect, mine to cherish.

In my darkest moments, I never thought I could feel

something like this. I never imagined that the walls around my heart could shatter so easily.

But this woman penetrated my defenses with a mere glance.

I'm so fucked.

21

RAVEN

Vinnie slides his fingers through my pussy folds, and I shudder. Is this really happening? Is he truly going to make love to my hairless body?

I want it.

I want all of it.

I want his head between my legs, his tongue inside me. I want his hands all over me, his lips all over me. I want that big hard cock inside me. Inside my mouth and inside my pussy.

He moves then, gets rid of the rest of his clothes in what seems like a flash, and I can't help a gasping gulp.

His masculine beauty is perfection. And that cock?

Massive is an understatement.

He says he's done with gentle?

Bring it on, Vinnie.

He steps closer, his silhouette large and looming over me. His eyes sear into mine, full of lust, raw passion, and a promise of pleasure. I squirm under his gaze, waiting for his touch again.

"Raven."

My name rolling off his tongue in that husky voice makes my knees weak.

I watch as he kneels down before me, his hands resting on my thighs. The pads of his fingers are rough as he trails up my skin, causing goosebumps to erupt in their wake.

With a swift move, Vinnie lifts one of my legs over his shoulder, parting me wide open for him. His hot breath fans over my pussy before he darts out his tongue to taste me. I shiver as I grip the sheets beneath me.

His mouth is magic. I'm lost in the way he laps at me, his movements anything but tender. I arch my back as the strong and heady pleasure hits me wave after wave.

He delves deeper, his fingers joining his mouth in their exploration. He strokes my inner walls and I gasp, the coil within me tightening further with each of his deft moves.

"Vinnie," I moan, the word a plea in the silence.

He raises his head, his gaze intense and full of promise. "You're mine," he says again with conviction.

The authority in his voice makes me shudder. Do I respond? No. He doesn't wait for a response. Instead he seals his lips over my clit and I cry out. His touch is all-consuming. His hands on my body are like fire against my skin while his mouth does wicked things to me that have my head spinning, my heart pounding.

His fingers are relentless, twisting and turning, amplifying the sensation while he sucks at my clit, licks it, releases, and then sucks hard on it once more. I clutch at the sheets, my knuckles white with the strain as I approach the edge.

"I'm close," I gasp out between heavy breaths.

Vinnie quickens his pace in response, his movements becoming more demanding.

"Let go," he commands, his voice husky and filled with longing. "Give it to me, Raven."

The spiral inside me snaps then, and I jolt with the force of my orgasm. Pleasure rips through me in waves, leaving me gasping and writhing beneath him. His name tumbles from my lips in both shouts and whispers as he continues his assault on me.

The pleasure continues to pulse through me again and again. Vinnie doesn't stop until I'm a trembling, sated mess beneath him.

As my orgasm recedes and I'm left breathless, he rises from between my legs, his eyes dark with desire, his lips glistening with my come. His gaze never leaves mine as he crawls up the length of my body, each muscle in his sculpted torso flexing with the effort.

He quickly unwraps a condom, sheaths himself, and positions his huge cock at my entrance, his hard length teasing me. I arch into him, aching with need. He captures my lips in a burning kiss even as he pushes inside me. He's so big, and I gasp at the intrusion, but then I open for him as he slides balls deep, filling me, easing the emptiness I've carried for so long.

"Raven," he groans. He locks his arms around me, cradling me close as he begins to move, slow at first, but then quickly, harshly.

Perfectly.

Each thrust sends a wave of pleasure crashing over me.

He pulls back slightly, aligning his hips with mine,

allowing him deeper access. I wrap my legs around him, pulling him closer and trying to fuse our bodies into one.

His movements become even faster, harder, matching the frantic beating of my heart. His muscles—shoulders, neck, upper arms—flex beautifully under the strain. He leans toward my neck, nipping and sucking on my skin.

With each thrust, he nudges my clit, and I'm on my way once more.

"Please..." I gasp out.

His thrusts become more erratic, losing their rhythm as he chases his own release.

"Yes..." he grunts. "Raven...you feel so good."

His words are like a match igniting gasoline. A wave of pleasure washes over me like a tsunami as I clench around him in another climax, pulling him deeper into me.

He follows me over the edge seconds later, my name ripping from his lips as he collapses on top of me, his body heavy and slick with sweat. We lie there, a tangled mess of limbs, gasping for breath as our mutual climaxes wind down.

The musky scent of sex—of us—fills the room. Vinnie trails lazy kisses along my sweaty neck, his soft puffs of breath fanning over my skin.

"Wow," he murmurs against my flesh.

"Vinnie," I whisper, turning slightly to press more fully into his solid warmth. I trace the contours of his muscled back and revel in the feel of him sprawled on top of me.

His answering hum is pure satisfaction. He pulls out slowly, drawing a low gasp from me at the sudden emptiness. He quickly discards the condom and returns, tugging me close again and wrapping his strong arms around me like a vise.

We lie in silence, our bodies intertwined. Vinnie traces idle patterns on my bare skin. I can feel the steady beat of his heart beneath my chest.

"Are you okay?" Vinnie asks.

"I'm more than okay," I assure him, pressing a tender kiss to his neck.

His body relaxes beneath me at my words, a sigh escaping his lips as he pulls me closer.

We lie there for what feels like hours, our bodies tangled together, our hearts beating in sync. I wrap my arms tighter around his waist, burying my face in the crook of his neck. His skin is warm and slightly salty from sweat, reminding me that what just transpired between us was real.

He slides his hand over my scalp, and for once, I don't think about my lack of hair. I simply hum in contentment and continue to press soft kisses to his collarbone.

"I've never known peace like this, Raven," he whispers into the silence. His confession sparks a warmth in my chest that spreads through me like wildfire.

"I know what you mean," I whisper back, looking up to meet his gaze.

Emotions swim in the depths of his eyes, a beautiful blend of love and fear, relief and uncertainty. It all mirrors my own feelings.

He traces my bottom lip. I part my lips slightly and brush my tongue against the pad of his thumb.

"I can't get enough of you," he says, an edge of desperation coating his voice.

"Then don't stop." I whisper back.

With a low growl, he rolls us over until I'm straddling

him, looking down into his dark eyes. He hands me a foil packet and I slide the condom over him.

He moves his hands to my hips, guiding me as I rise and fall on his length at a slow but steady rhythm. His gaze never leaves mine as I move on him, slowly this time, each gasp and sigh echoing in the quiet room. He reaches out to cup my cheek, and I turn into his palm and lightly kiss it.

He said he doesn't do gentle, but this is gentle. The calm after the storm.

The heat of his gaze, the sensation of his body beneath mine, the rhythm of our mingled breaths in the silent room —all of it combines to a singular overwhelming sense of ecstasy that leaves me teetering on the brink once again, just a heartbeat away from tumbling over.

"And again," Vinnie groans, his voice strained with effort and steeped in raw emotion.

"Again," I echo, my voice a breathy whisper.

Vinnie grasps my hips tighter, and he moves me up and down on him forcefully. Soon I'm nearing the peak again. Our movements become disjointed and erratic, bodies straining for that explosive release once more. Our gasps and moans fill the room as we chase after it together.

Finally, we crest over the edge in unison. My climax, fierce and beautiful, rips through me, leaving me panting. Vinnie buries himself deep within me one last time before stilling, his body racked with tremors.

Heaving for breath, we collapse against each other, bodies slick with sweat. The intensity of the moment fades into a quiet satisfaction, a blissful peace that seeps into my very bones.

As I lie on top of him, my head resting on his chest rising

and falling with his labored breaths, I feel something otherworldly.

I'm not in love.

I couldn't be.

I hardly know this man. He hardly knows me. But it's something. Something that could grow.

His hand is soft on my skin, his fingers tracing lazy circles on my scalp.

"Vinnie," I begin, but the words catch in my throat, refusing to form. The silence stretches between us.

He tilts my chin up, his dark eyes boring into mine. The moonlight dances in their depths, revealing a vulnerability I didn't see before. A softness that tugs at something deep within me.

"What is it?" he asks, his voice a low murmur.

I hesitate for a moment, searching his gaze. Can I tell him what I'm feeling? Can I put into words this strange connection that seems to bind us together?

"I feel ...something," I admit, my voice barely audible.

He meets my gaze but says nothing.

And I'm okay with that.

He doesn't need to say anything.

What we just did said it all.

22

VINNIE

My body is sated, and my heart...

Raven said she feels something. I also feel something.

Something I have no business feeling.

But once I finally come down from my release, the emotion I dread swoops in.

Guilt.

Fucking guilt.

I took advantage of Raven, of her vulnerability.

She's healing from leukemia, for God's sake.

I close my eyes, feeling the weight of this transgression like lead in the pit of my stomach. My hands, still holding onto Raven's frail body, feel heavier. Culpability gnaws at me, tearing at the edges of my consciousness.

Fucking guilt. It's a monster that never sleeps, awakening at the most inconvenient of times.

Raven stirs beside me, her eyes fluttering open to meet mine. Rings of exhaustion are painted around them, but she manages to smile.

"Are you okay?" she asks.

I want to scream, tell her I'm far from okay. Admit my guilt and beg for her forgiveness. But how can I burden her with this? How can I add to the turmoil she must already be feeling?

Instead, I force a nod. "Of course I'm okay. That was amazing."

"I agree." Her smile is a dazzling one.

Again, the guilt threatens to eat me away from the inside out.

I have to kill a man, and I just made love to the most beautiful, sweet, and vulnerable woman in the world.

I give her a chaste kiss on her forehead. "I need to get going. I have an early meeting."

Not exactly a lie. I have to check in with my grandfather every morning. It's a pain in the ass, but it's the life I chose to return to.

She wraps her arms around me. "You don't have to go."

God, if only…

If only I could stay, embedded in the peace and solace I find in her body.

But I can't.

This thing between us never should have happened. What I'm feeling for this woman—this woman I barely know—isn't right.

I'm lost. Completely lost.

I look at this beautiful woman. This beautiful woman with her dark peach fuzz, her barely visible eyelashes and eyebrows. And yes, while she certainly is beautiful, lust for her alone is not what drew me to her.

Not too many people lust after women who have lost all their hair due to cancer treatments.

I kiss her again, this time on the lips, but I resist the urge to slide my tongue between hers. "I'm sorry. But I do have to go."

She moves away from me, ready to slide off the bed, but I stop her. "Don't get up. I can see myself out."

She yawns, stretching her arms above her as she sits on the edge of the bed. "But I do. I need to go back to my mom and dad's house. They'll worry otherwise. They may have already called Falcon and Savannah to see where I am."

"You didn't text them?"

She shrugs. "I guess I forgot. I was focused on...something else."

I can't help a churlish grin. "So they're keeping tabs on you, huh?"

"Yes and no." She frowns. "I mean, yes they are. Because of what I've been through, they're worried about me. But normally they wouldn't. We were all raised to be strong and confident people, independent people."

"I understand. They're just concerned. They don't want to take any chance of losing you."

"I know."

"I'll drive you to your parents' house."

"You sure you don't mind?"

Is she kidding? At this moment, I'd buy the moon for her if I could. "No, I don't mind."

"The good news is that it's on the way. You won't have to go out of your way like you did to get here."

I chuckle lightly as I stroke the length of her arm. "Raven, none of that matters to me. I'll take you to your parents' house. Then I'll go home to Austin. I'll be home by about two a.m. Trust me. I've gotten by on much less sleep."

"You know what?" She swings her feet to the side of the bed. "You don't even need to do that. I can text my mom now and tell her I'm staying with Falcon."

"No. If anything happened to you while you were here alone, I could never forgive myself." I grab her hand and squeeze it. "Don't lie to your mom, Raven. Don't lie period—even when it seems like a simple white lie. Because lies? They tend to mushroom. One lie begets another bigger one. It just keeps growing."

She looks at me, her lips parted. "Vinnie? You okay?"

I nod, knowing full well my affirmation is a lie. I'm so far from okay. But I won't add to her weight to bear.

What I said about lying is true. I saw lies in action growing up. I'll continue to see them now. Now that I've come back to the family fold. The lies will grow, just as my duties will grow.

Killing Giacomo Puzo is just the beginning. I'll kill others.

Others I have no personal beef with.

I'll kill if I have to.

And one day...

I'll kill my own damned grandfather.

23

RAVEN

Vinnie and I get dressed in silence, and I can't help but notice that my panties are no longer wearable. No big deal. I throw them in the trash can next to my bathroom and slide on my jeans commando.

Such a stark difference from when we undressed. That was quick and frantic and primal.

Now we're acting as if we're dressing to get ready to go to work. Slowly and methodically.

And silently.

I hope Vinnie doesn't regret what happened between us, because I certainly don't. The sex was phenomenal, and it was with a man who is probably the most handsome man I've ever laid eyes on—and that's saying a lot considering my brothers are all extremely good-looking and I've had more than a few boyfriends who were *bona fide* hotties.

Vinnie Gallo is in a category all by himself.

He could be walking runways in New York and Paris, modeling the latest fashions from top designers.

It's funny that he doesn't look a lot like Savannah. They

have something of a sibling resemblance, but Savannah's skin is fair, and she has a spray of freckles across her nose. She's pretty in a best-friend's-sister kind of way. I have no idea what their other brother looked like—and I could never ask to see a picture. That would be bringing up memories for Vinnie and Savannah that I'm sure are better left buried.

But Vinnie himself...

He makes those men on *People Magazine's* "Sexiest Man Alive" covers look average.

And his body...

Damn.

Shoulders so broad and muscular and a chest so hard, with nipples like dark brown coins that respond every time I touch them.

His abs. The perfect sixpack, leading to a black bush framing a big beautiful cock.

His ass—perfectly formed and leading to hard thighs and thick calves and big feet with perfect square nails.

There's just nothing wrong with that man at all.

And he wanted *me*.

Granted, I was considered quite a beauty in my day, but right now I'm thin. Too thin. And I have no hair.

But for some reason, Vinnie wanted me. I will be thinking about this encounter with him long after today.

I'll also be breaking that date with Brick Latham.

Not that I expect Vinnie to ask me out. But it wouldn't be fair to Brick when my thoughts are elsewhere.

Maybe I'll call CJ. She wants to get together on Sunday, but I'd like to see her before then. I'm not supposed to be driving, but I can always take a rideshare or a cab. Maybe I could get Mom to drive me, although driving all the way into an Austin suburb is a two-hour project.

I'll take a rideshare.

When we're finally dressed, Vinnie reaches his hand to me, and I take it. We walk in silence through my house to the doorway, where he opens it for me. I lock up, and we walk to the car where he opens the passenger-side door for me.

The drive is silent as well, save for me telling him where to turn to get to my parents' house.

When he finally pulls into the driveway, the gravel crunching beneath the tires of his car, he turns off the engine and looks at me. "I want you to know that I wish I could see you again," he says.

My eyes widen as my heart sinks to my tummy. "So you're saying you *won't* see me again?"

He closes his eyes and leans over the steering wheel. "It's not that I don't want to, Raven. I could say tonight shouldn't have happened, but we both know that would be a lie. I wanted it. I took what wasn't mine to take."

I place my hand over his. "You didn't take anything, Vinnie. I gave myself to you, and I'd do it again."

He smiles, but it's a sad smile. "You're so beautiful. So sweet and good." He looks into my eyes for a moment and then casts his gaze to the floor of his car. "And I'm..."

"I know what you do for a living, Vinnie. It's not like I went into this blind."

He doesn't reply at first. Simply licks his full lips, looks out the windshield, and then back to me. "Tonight meant more to me than I can even find words to describe," he says. "Thank you."

I shake my head. "Thank you? I don't think anyone's ever thanked me for sex before."

"I'm not thanking you for the sex, Raven, although it was fantastic."

I smile. "It was."

I expect him to continue, but when he doesn't, I prompt him. "What exactly are you thanking me for then?"

He lets out a sigh and rakes his fingers through his hair. "I'm thanking you for being you. And for allowing me to escape, if only for an hour or two."

His words clamp around my heart like a fist. "So that's what you're saying? That I was only an escape to you?"

"Fuck no!" He shakes his head. "That's not what I'm saying at all. You are so much more than escape. You are someone I could..."

"You could what?"

He takes a deep breath in and then sighs. "I can't allow myself to go there. Not with what I have in front of me. But maybe someday, Raven. Maybe someday."

"Vinnie, what exactly are you getting at?"

He looks at me then. Really *looks* at me with those dark eyes. I swear to God he has X-ray vision, and he's seeing straight into my heart. "What I'm saying is this can't happen again. As much as I want it—and I do want it, Raven—I'm not good for you. We both know that."

I cross my arms. "Who are you to decide what's good for me? Isn't that *my* decision?"

"Of course it is. But it's my decision as well. And I'm afraid it can't go on."

I scoff. "Whatever. If you're intent on punishing yourself for some unknown crime by keeping yourself from something that you want, far be it from me to change your mind." I unclick the door and begin walking to the house.

When I get to the door, I expect for Vinnie to be behind me. I expect a hug. A kiss. I expect something.

But the man who has been a consummate gentleman all night is still seated in his car.

He stays. His headlights light the lawn, and I realize he's waiting for me to get inside safely.

He's not coming back.

I push the key into the door and walk inside my parents' house. I go to the kitchen, pour myself a large glass of water, go to my room, take my medication, go to the bathroom, and then lie down in my bed.

And I cry myself to sleep.

IN THE MORNING, I sleep in for a few hours. When I finally make my way to the bathroom to take a shower, I'm disgusted by the look on my face.

My eyes are puffy, and my nose is red from the crying I did last night over Vinnie Gallo.

Believe it or not, it's been a while since I've cried.

When I was first diagnosed, I bawled my eyes out. So did Mom, and even Dad shed some tears. Hawk, Eagle, and Robin all cried as well.

And Falcon?

Well, he was in prison, so I don't know if he cried. I couldn't visit him to tell him the news. I had Hawk tell him.

And I never asked Hawk what my older brother's reaction was.

I couldn't take it.

I cried my eyes out that first night. Then I realized that crying wasn't going to help me. The only thing that would help me was *me*. I had to get into a fighting mindset, and my God, there were times I wanted to throw in the towel. Times I wanted to slit my wrists just to be done with the pain.

But I didn't.

I fought.

I took every small step I could take on the road to recovery, and even when I was told, after the worst round of chemo yet, that I wasn't in remission and the only chance was a bone marrow transplant, I still didn't cry.

Why should I? I had four siblings. One of them was bound to be a match.

And one of them was.

The transplant worked. I'm in remission. My hair is growing back. I feel...*good*.

How many people in the world must take for granted how good actually feels?

Because when you don't feel good? All you want is to feel normal again. Even those days when you're only a little bit sick, and you don't feel perfect... When you're chronically ill with a catastrophic illness, you beg for those days.

I get into the shower, scrub my face clean, and then, when I'm done washing my hair and my body, I turn the shower to cold.

And I stand there.

Letting the cold water pelt me.

It will ease the swelling of my eyelids, ease the redness on my face.

Because you know what it also does?

It wakes me up.

It resets me, as if I'm a computer.

Back to normal Raven. The Raven who is grateful for her second chance at life.

Raven, who would never cry over a man.

Once I'm out of the shower and dried off, I dress in black leggings and an oversized white sweatshirt. When I look in the mirror, I realize my legs look too thin. What the hell? Leggings are comfortable, and I like them. My legs will fill out. I've been eating well.

For the first time in a while, I actually apply some blush and a light color of lipstick.

No mascara, of course, because I don't have eyelashes yet. But even with my peach-fuzz head, when I look in the mirror, I see some remnants of what I used to look like.

My cheeks are not as hollow as they were. And they'll continue to fill out.

Though my legs are thin, I see they're shapely.

I see the Raven I used to be.

I'll never *be* that same Raven, but I will look like her again. It won't take as long as it seems.

I head down, and Mom is in the kitchen cleaning up from breakfast. "Hey," she says. "You got back from Falcon's pretty late last night."

Except I wasn't at Falcon's. "Yeah, we had some nice talks. That's why I slept in a little."

Mom dries a plate and places it in the cupboard. "You should be sleeping, Ray. You know none of us expect you to be up before dawn like the rest of us."

"I want to be. I want to be part of the family again. I want to get back to normal."

Mom frowns. "Don't force it, Raven. You're still healing."

She's not wrong, and she's right that I shouldn't force it. But last night...

My mother has no idea what I did last night, but it took a lot of strength, and I was glad to use it.

Even if Vinnie doesn't want to see me again...

Nope. Not going there. I don't want to start bawling again.

But already I know I won't.

Because even though I'm not sick anymore—thank God—my mindset is the same. Crying doesn't do anyone any good. So no longer will I cry over Vinnie Gallo.

"Can I make you some breakfast?" Mom asks.

"Maybe just two scrambled eggs and a piece of toast," I say.

"Coming right up." I clear my throat. "I think I'll go to Austin today to see CJ."

Mom raises an eyebrow. "Have you been cleared to drive yet?"

"No, but I'll just call an Uber."

"That's an awful long Uber ride. I can take you."

I shake my head. "That would take your whole day. Dad needs you here. I can take an Uber. I'll be home by suppertime."

"If you're sure." Mom grabs some eggs and bread out of the fridge.

"I'm sure, but thanks for the offer, Mommy."

I see her back quiver a bit when I use the word "mommy." It's what we all called her when we were kids, but once we hit our teens, we never used it anymore. So she gets a little emotional on the rare occasion that we do.

A few minutes later, she slides my breakfast in front of me, along with a cup of coffee and a glass of orange juice.

I'm not a big orange juice fan—my love of Orange Crush notwithstanding—but I drink it. I drink it because my mother thinks it's the most nutritious beverage in the world, even though, like most fruit juice, it's full of sugar. It's also full of vitamins, I guess, so I'll give her this one.

Once I'm back at my own place, I'll be nixing the OJ.

I eat my breakfast quickly, even though I'm not very hungry. Not that I lost my appetite or anything. I ate a huge piece of lasagna last night at Falcon and Savannah's place.

I'm just a little bummed about the way Vinnie left things.

I force myself to eat because I know I'll feel better soon. I don't let myself feel bad anymore.

Once I'm done with my breakfast, Mom collects my plate and empty glass of OJ, and she gives me a smile, leaving me with my coffee. I grab my phone to text CJ.

I'm coming into Austin today and would love to see you. Lunch?

She texts me right back.

Thought you couldn't drive.

I'm calling an Uber.

Perf! Actually today is a great day. The kids are at school, and I have very few chores for Mrs. P. Come to the house and I'll make us a delicious lunch. This house has so much food in it, and I'm allowed to use whatever I want.

She's okay with you having guests?

Absolutely. At least while the kids aren't home. When they're home, she's pretty clear that they're my priority, but she also made it clear that her home is my home, and I should feel free to have friends over. Just no overnight guests.

Great. I'm going to catch an Uber soon and I'll let you know when I'm on my way.

Fabulous. I'll see what I can pull together for lunch. Can't wait to see you!

I text back a smiley emoji and then turn back to Mom. "I'm going to order my Uber. It'll be a long drive, so I'm going to go ahead and get moving."

"All right, Raven. If you need anything at all, you know who to call."

"I know. Thanks." I rise, take my cup of coffee, and head back to my room, where I pull up the Uber app to order a ride. It usually takes at least a half hour to get an Uber to come into the ranch, and just as I suspected, today is no different. I have forty-five minutes before the driver arrives, so I settle in with my cup of coffee, and I grab a book off my shelf.

But I stare at the pages, the words never reaching my brain.

I'm lost in fantasy about last night.

And Vinnie Gallo.

24

VINNIE

I sit in my grandfather's office, looking him straight in his bloodshot brown eyes.

I've seen pictures of my grandfather when he was younger.

He's nearly a dead ringer for me.

I always hated that, especially after he brutally violated me when I was eighteen.

He and I have the same olive skin, the same dark hair. His eyes are the same color as mine, but even in his youth, his held a dark coldness that no picture of mine can match. Even after everything I've been through—and I've been through a lot, especially during my time abroad—I still see a little life, a little goodness, in my eyes every morning when I look in the mirror. I'm determined not to let that die out like my grandfather did.

Mikey always looked more like my father. Savannah favors him as well. Hair that's not quite as dark, eyes not quite as brown, fairer skin.

But me?

Except for my eyes—God willing—I'm looking in a mirror at myself in fifty years.

And I don't like what I see.

"Grandfather," I say, "do you remember when I was seventeen and I walked in on you and Dad meeting with some drug kingpin named Diego Vega?"

"Of course I do." Grandfather chuckles. "Vega."

I furrow my brow. "Do you find that amusing?"

He strokes his chin. "Not amusing so much as a bit nostalgic. Your father and I considered him an ally at one point, but he turned out to be a bad seed."

"Oh?" I cock my head.

"He ended up fucking up a huge deal, and his men mutinied on him. He got demoted to overseeing a bunch of lowlife pushers." His eyes sparkle deviously. "His work got sloppy, so we had him taken care of."

I hold my jaw in place, but it wants to drop.

My grandfather took credit for Vega's demise?

Motherfucker...

I keep my face noncommittal.

"I see. What did he do to piss you off?"

"This happened eight years ago," Grandfather says. "What does it matter?"

"If I'm going to take over for you," I say, "don't I need to know what someone did to earn your disfavor?"

Grandfather looks up at me and a small grin spreads over his face. A grin reeking of malice, of sadism, of...pride, perhaps?

"He was a hothead," Grandfather says. "He could no longer be trusted." He slowly returns his gaze to me. "Why the sudden interest in this man, Vincent?"

Hothead? Seems accurate. Only a hothead would give a damn about a low-level pusher like Eagle Bellamy. A true boss would leave it to his minions. Something about Eagle Bellamy irked Vega and he couldn't stay out of it. If he had, he might still be alive today.

Or maybe not, if my grandfather wanted him gone.

Hothead. If there's one thing I can say about my grandfather, it's that he's *not* a hothead. He's cool and calculating.

Which is how I need to play him now.

"It matters to me," I say. "If you expect me to take care of people when they screw us over, I need to know why you took care of Vega."

"Why Vega?"

I comb my brain for a believable lie. "He's just a man I remember from the past," I say. "He called me 'little cobra.' I never understood that."

"Because it's what *I* called you," Grandfather says.

I furrow my brow once more. "Never in your life did you call me 'little cobra.'"

He chuckles. "Not to your face. But that's how I referred to you in the organization. The little cobra. The one who would take over for me eventually. The one who would one day lead the family in my absence." His gaze darkens. "I had a lot of clean-up to do when you disappeared. All I heard from Vega was 'the cobra didn't grow up. Where's your pride and joy? Little cobra is more like little garter snake.'"

I didn't think I could possibly hate a dead man, but I absently feel my hands curl into fists. And I'm damned glad Vega is cold and dead in the ground, put there by Eagle Bellamy, because I'd like to wring his neck.

I never understood Vega's cobra comment, but I did look

up the traditional traits of the snake when I was overseas. I wanted to know what Vega saw in me. According to what I read, cobras are intelligent and territorial, certainly a good trait for the heir to our unseemly dynasty. Above all, they project confidence when threatened by expanding the ribs in their necks to create a hood. In a business where appearances can be everything, that matters a lot.

I'll admit, I am a poster child for each of those traits. But I will use every single cobra attribute I possess not to lead this organization, but to burn it all to the fucking ground.

Grandfather is lying to me. If he had ever referred to me as "little cobra," I would know it. He's also lying about who killed Vega. And I have a feeling that this is just the tip of the iceberg.

Damn it all. Did Eagle Bellamy do my grandfather a huge favor years ago without even knowing it?

"What did Vega do to merit his demise?" I ask.

Grandfather folds his hands together. "He made a costly mistake."

"What was that mistake?"

Grandfather shakes his head. "You expect me to remember every little mistake somebody I work with has made? I could fill a couple volumes."

"Does every mistake merit being"—air quote—"*taken care of?*"

He burns me with his gaze. "Don't take this lightly, Vincent."

"Who's taking anything lightly?"

"When you use that tone and make air quotes, you're taking it lightly. What we do is business, pure and simple. And it's *never* to be taken lightly." Grandfather darts his gaze—just his eyes—to the left and back. So quickly that I may not have noticed if I hadn't been staring at him so tightly.

He's lying. I already know that. I know that because he didn't have Vega taken care of.

Unless...

Unless he knew...

No.

My grandfather has no interest in the names of the scumbags selling drugs on the street.

There's no way he knows about Eagle Bellamy.

But somehow Myra at the EPA already knew...

"Enough about this shit," Grandfather says. "Where are we on Puzo?"

"Working on it," I say.

"Are you? Because I looked into it last evening, and Giacomo Puzo and his wife were both at home, their two children tucked into bed."

"Did you want me to just march right into his house and shoot him?" I ask.

Grandfather shrugs. "I gave you the fucking gun, didn't I?"

"Yeah, you did." I stare him down. "But I'll do this my way. I'll prove to you once and for all, Grandfather, that I'm as loyal to this family as I've ever been."

He stares me straight in the eye. "You're not scared, are you, Vinnie? You can walk right into his home and shoot him dead. I'll have everything fixed for you."

"I know that." I keep my voice steady, looking him straight in the eye.

But the truth of the matter is that I *don't* know that. And I'm not going to off Puzo until I'm convinced of one thing.

My grandfather's so concerned about whether he can trust me.

I'm a hundred times more concerned about trusting *him*.

I've seen what he is capable of.

I'm not convinced he didn't have a hand in Mikey's death.

So yeah, I don't trust that he'll have everything fixed.

And the fact that he's taking credit for Diego Vega?

He proved to me what I've always known.

He's a fucking criminal and a fucking liar.

And I'm taking him out.

25

RAVEN

"Oh my God, Ray, your gorgeous hair!"

I'm shocked by CJ's reaction when she answers the door to the mansion in the Austin suburb.

Until—

She looks me up and down and her jaw drops. "Oh my God... You had sex, didn't you?"

"How am I supposed to give you shit about mentioning my hair when you follow up with that?" I walk in through the door that CJ holds open into a foyer that puts my house to shame.

A gorgeous golden retriever nudges me for pets. I slide my hand over his silky head. "What's your name?"

"That's Francis," CJ says.

"You're a good boy, aren't you?" I look around. "My God... This place is a freaking mansion."

She cocks her head. "You're one to talk. You live in a mansion."

"I live in a sprawling ranch house. It's not the same thing."

CJ closes the door and leans in. "So who is he?"

My chest warms. "Who's who?"

"The guy you had sex with. It's written all over your face."

This is really bizarre. CJ and I haven't seen each other in how many years? And she thinks she knows that I had sex?

The fact that she's right...

I swallow. "I didn't have sex, CJ."

CJ furrows her brow. "I can always tell. It's my superpower."

"Then your superpower is off today."

"Okay... If you say so, Ray." CJ purses her lips. "Maybe your new hairstyle threw me. What moved you to chop it all off?"

I run my hands over my scalp. Guess there's no more avoiding the subject. I forgot how blunt CJ can be.

"Actually, it wasn't my choice," I say. "I'm recovering from cancer."

CJ slaps her hand over her mouth. "Oh my God, Ray, I had no idea. I'm so sorry."

I shake my head. "Please don't make a big deal out of it. I would have told you over the phone, but I..."

She nods slowly. "I told you that my dad had just died from cancer and you didn't want to double bum me out."

"That, and it just seemed like something I should tell you in person. Sorry if I gave you a shock."

She cracks an uneasy smile. "And I'm sorry for being a dumbass. Assuming you shaved your gorgeous head of hair for the aesthetic."

"Are you suggesting I can't pull it off?" I ask. "I could always start a death metal band, purchase an all-leather wardrobe, really embrace the whole thing."

That gets a laugh out of her. "Glad to see the chemo didn't take out your sense of humor." She leans in, her eyes narrowing. "I'm still convinced you had sex."

Damn, she's good.

"Who would want to have sex with me in this condition?"

"Cancer patients can have sex."

I can't help bursting into laughter at that one. She's the same old Ceej. Instead of asking me about my cancer, she's more concerned with my sex life.

And honestly, I'm happy to not dwell on the last few years of misery.

"What's so funny?" she asks.

"Cancer patients are doing what they can to stay alive. They're usually so ill from treatment that sex is the last thing on their mind."

She wiggles her eyebrows. "Well, it's obviously on your mind, because you had sex, Raven. Don't try to tell me you didn't."

I roll my eyes. "This isn't high school anymore, Ceej. That doesn't work."

She purses her lips. "Your cheeks are flushed, you have a permanent smile on your face, and you just look... I don't know... Satisfied."

I force myself to frown. "I *am* satisfied. I spent the last couple years fighting for my life, and I'm in remission now. My brother's bone marrow worked. I'm going to be okay. I'm going to live a long life. I'm absolutely thrilled about that. I think you might just be mistaking the fact that I'm ecstatic to be alive for something else."

She tilts her head, regards me, studies me.

Silence reigns for a few moments, and just when I'm sure she's not going to say another thing—

"Maybe..." She crosses her arms and smirks. "I still think you had sex though."

"Do you honestly think a guy would have me without a head of hair?"

"Raven, you've always been gorgeous. Having no hair doesn't change that. So you lost a few pounds too. So what? I don't look like you on my best day."

That's a crock, and CJ knows it. She's a beautiful woman, with reddish-brown hair and amazing hazel eyes. She's not as tall as I am, and slightly curvier, but I have basically no curves right now because of all the weight I've lost. They'll return, but I've never been hugely curvy. I'm long and lean with a flat belly and good-sized breasts. "You're just as gorgeous as I am, we both know it. So show me around this mansion of yours."

"God, I wish it were mine." She looks around the foyer. "It belongs to this richer-than-God family. The dad is some high-powered lawyer, and he's hardly ever home. He travels a lot. The mom doesn't work, but she's always got something going all day. Whether it's a meeting of the Junior League, the school board, some kind of charity event... She's never home. The kids are in private school, and I take them in the morning and pick them up and then make sure they get a snack."

"You mean you don't cook them dinner too?"

She shrugs. "Sometimes I have to. I make a mean box of mac and cheese. But the housekeeper usually does that. Her name is Marian. But I think today's her day off. I haven't seen her around."

"They've got a full-time nanny and a full-time housekeeper?"

"Yeah, and the dad has a full-time driver too."

"Damn."

She strokes her chin. "Not a lot different from how you grew up."

I gaze out a large living-room window. "I suppose not."

She's right in that we never had to worry about money. Our ranch is very successful, but our real money comes from my father's mother, Sandra Cooper Bellamy, the Cooper Steel heiress. She passed away while Falcon was in prison. He was able to come to the funeral on furlough, but then he had to go back.

That was a little over a year ago.

She was never the same once Falcon went away. I just thought it was her age, but now that I know that Falcon went to her for the money Eagle needed, I realize that she must have been utterly brokenhearted. She went to her grave thinking that she was responsible for her grandson's imprisonment. If only there were a way to tell her that Falcon was just trying to do right by his family.

All that money couldn't save her from dying in sorrow. Money can't save you from a lot of things. I still got cancer, still nearly died. Falcon still went to jail. Eagle still got involved in a drug ring.

Hawk and Robin seem to be okay, but who the hell knows anymore?

But now isn't the time to think about this. I'm catching up with an old friend.

"Let's have a look around anyway," I say.

"Not until you tell me about what you've been through," she says. "I'm so sorry, Ray."

I shrug. "Please, don't be. I'm going to be fine, and for that I'm truly grateful. I could tell you all about it, but it will make me sound like a Debbie Downer. I try to dwell on the fact that I got through it and made it to the other side."

"That's amazing," CJ says. "I wish I'd been here to help."

I shake my head. "I had my family. My brothers and sister. And frankly I wasn't big on other visitors. But let's talk about something else. Show me around this fabulous house."

CJ flashes a smile. "Gladly. Follow me."

CJ's employers' mansion is about the same size as my parents', but while the Bellamys built their home with the express purpose of raising a family in mind, these people seem to have designed their home with nothing but pure lavishness as the main objective. CJ takes me to the home theater adorned with rich velvet drapes and outfitted with plush reclining seats, surround sound, and even an old-fashioned popcorn maker. Then she shows me the indoor pool, complete with lounge chairs, a luxurious cedar sauna, and a jetted jacuzzi.

Onward to the library, the billiard room—I feel like I'm playing a game of *Clue*—and we finish out the tour in the music room, which is bedecked with a nine-foot Steinway grand piano, acoustic and electric guitars, a violin, and a drum set.

"Do your employers play a lot of music?" I ask. "They nearly have an entire orchestra in this room alone."

CJ scoffs. "Not a one. People like this own musical instruments because they're *supposed* to, not because they actually use them." She giggles and punches me in the arm. "Get with the program, Ray."

I laugh, but seeing this room full of beautiful instruments cursed to a life of complete silence makes me a little sad.

"But I still have to show you the best part," CJ goes on. "Follow me."

She leads me to a closed door on the mansion's third floor.

"This," she says, opening the door, "is my room."

I nearly drop my jaw. It's gorgeous. CJ has a king-sized bed with a tufted headboard upholstered in a cream-colored fabric. The bed itself is covered in what I think are silk sheets in a sweet baby blue. Flanking her bed are matching nightstands made of dark wood, each topped with a sleek, modern lamp. A large mirror hangs above an antique wooden dresser. A comfortable reading nook sits on one side of the room, featuring a plush armchair upholstered in a muted floral fabric beside a small bookshelf filled with an array of romance novels—CJ's favorite. She used to read them all the time back in school. The walls are painted the same color as her bedsheets, enhanced by elegant crown molding, and are adorned with a few serene watercolor landscapes depicting tranquil countryside scenes, as well as a striking abstract piece in shades of blue and gold.

I walk up to the abstract piece and notice the autograph in the bottom right corner. "Is this a genuine Roy Wolfe painting?"

CJ shrugs. "Who knows? I doubt these people would buy prints."

"Did they let you decorate yourself?"

She bursts out laughing. "Oh God no. Are you kidding?

This place has all been professionally decorated. And believe it or not, this is the smallest room in the house. But I have my own bathroom, and it's closer to the kids' rooms than the master is, of course, because if the kids get up in the night with a problem, guess who's supposed to come to their aid?"

"Well...you are their nanny."

"I am, and they pay me very well for what I do. I like the kids a lot, and I don't mind. But it's just..." She shakes her head. "These people are the most hands-off parents I've ever seen, and you know how I grew up."

CJ's dad was in the military and was gone a lot, and her mother worked full time, so she barely had one parent for most of her childhood. She spent a lot of time at my house, hanging with Robin and me.

She leads me into her bathroom, which is decadent. It almost looks like a master bathroom, with a jetted tub, separate shower, and a double vanity.

"I guess you're pretty comfortable here," I say.

"Yeah." She sits on the side of the tub. "I was really lucky to land this gig. I get to keep most of my salary because my room and board are paid for. They even gave me use of a car, you know, to drive the kids around."

"Do they let you use it for private purposes?"

She beams. "They sure do. On my day off, I can use it to go wherever I want. That's how I'll get to your place on Sunday."

"Sounds like a dream job," I say.

"It is, except I only get one day off a week. Every other day, I'm on call twenty-four-seven. But it's not that bad, really, because the kids are at school for eight hours. I don't have to clean or cook—the housekeeper does that. My job is just the kids."

"That's awesome, Ceej. I'm happy for you."

"Thanks." She grabs me and hugs me. "It's just so good to see you, Ray. How did we lose touch?"

"I don't know. You were in Germany, for one."

"I know." Her face falls. "My bad."

"It's not all your fault." I lay a hand on her arm. "I could've reached out and I didn't. Although the last couple of years I've been kind of busy."

"I totally understand." She grabs my hands. "So it's for sure that you're cured?"

"Well, nothing's ever a hundred percent sure," I tell her, "but they're very optimistic. My body has reacted really well to Falcon's bone marrow, so well that they let me go home a few days after the transplant. I've been recovering at home. At my parents' home actually. They didn't want me staying alone. But I've got to tell you, I can't wait to get back to my place full-time."

"So you can have sex?" CJ giggles.

I roll my eyes at her. "You have not changed one bit, Ceej. It gives a little sense of constancy in my universe. I might not be able to trust my own blood cells, but I can trust that you'll be the same goblin I grew up with. It's so great to see you."

She gives me a hug. "You too, Ray."

CJ takes me through the rest of the house, and we end up in the large gourmet kitchen. I grew up with a large gourmet kitchen. My mom is a great cook, and oftentimes we had housekeepers to help with the cooking as well. But make no mistake about it. The kitchen was my mother's domain, and she made sure every housekeeper understood that. I bet Mrs. Whatever-Her-Name-Is never set foot in this kitchen.

Plus, our kitchen is nearly a century old. It's been updated, of course, but it has a lot of old country charm. This one? Totally different. It's monochromatic, sterile-looking, with a huge Viking stove and polished stainless-steel appliances. The counters look like marble, and there are not one, not two, but five sinks in this kitchen.

"What on earth do they need five sinks for?"

"Oh, I have this one memorized," CJ says. "One is for food prep, one is for baking prep, to avoid cross contamination, of course." She rolls her eyes. "The one in the butler's pantry is for prepping dishes and glassware for formal dinners." She walks over to the wet bar. "This one of course is for rinsing drinkware for the bar, and that big one in the back"—she points—"is for cleanup. Pots and pans and the like."

"Wow," is all I can say.

"Right?" CJ sighs. "If I enjoyed cooking more, I could have a field day in here."

"You can use the whole house then?"

"Yeah. Except the master bedroom. They keep it locked when they're home."

I shrug a moment. "I guess that makes sense."

"You think so?"

"Yeah. I mean, if they have expensive jewelry in there or something."

"Oh, they wouldn't have that. They keep all of that kind of stuff in the safe. It's in the family room, behind the gun cabinet."

I grew up around guns. I learned to shoot when I was a

kid. So the fact that CJ mentioned a gun cabinet shouldn't make the back of my neck go cold.

But for some reason, it does.

I shrug it off.

My body doesn't react the same way it used to before I was sick. Things change. So much poison was pumped into me, my nerves don't react the way they normally do.

That's all this is, obviously.

"Why wouldn't they want you going into their room then?"

She shrugs. "Heck if I know. They're probably just private. But who cares? I have no desire to see their room anyway. I mean, like what if they're into bondage or something?" She lets out a shudder.

I laugh. "That could be one reason they don't want you in there."

"Though I doubt it," she says. "Mrs. P is about as uptight as they get. The pearl-clutching kind of uptight, if you know what I mean."

I nod. "Yup. I'm familiar."

CJ crosses the large kitchen to the fridge and opens it, scanning its contents. "I've got all kinds of things we can whip up for lunch. I'm not a huge cook, as I said, but Marian made some awesome chicken salad last night for dinner. There are leftovers, and it will be great on some sourdough bread. I can add some lettuce and tomato. And there's some chips. Plus Diet Coke. Does that sound good?"

I glance inside the refrigerator. "Do you happen to have Orange Crush?"

She clamps her hand over her mouth. "Oh my God, Ray. Are you still drinking that stuff?"

I smile. "Tastes just like sunshine."

She moves some items in the fridge around, frowning. "I wish I had a can for you. I remember you stocked your dorm room minifridge to the brim with it. All I've got is some bottled water and Diet Coke. There might be some apple juice or orange juice. Would OJ be a good substitute?"

I chuckle. "Tastes too real. I need the artificial, neon-dyed goodness that is Orange Crush. But

Diet Coke or water is fine." I smile at her.

"Go ahead and take a seat at the counter there. I'll get our sandwiches made."

I sit at the island, admiring the gorgeous marble countertop streaked in black and gold. "I can't get over how gorgeous this marble is," I say.

"Oh yeah. Apparently they had it imported from Italy. One giant slab that they cut to size. Incredible, isn't it?"

"Yeah. I mean, my mom has gorgeous granite countertops in her kitchen, but this is something else entirely."

"I know." CJ slices off several slices of bread from a golden-brown loaf and heaps chicken salad on top of each one. She adds some crisp lettuce and a few slices of tomato. "You want onion?"

"No, thanks."

"Good enough." She slices a few thin slivers of red onion onto her own sandwich but leaves mine alone.

She sets them on the counter, sliding mine in front of me along with a snack-size bag of chips and a can of Diet Coke. "Bon appétit," she says.

I grab a napkin from the napkin holder on the counter and place it in my lap. Then I take a bite of the sandwich. "Wow, it's delicious. So crunchy."

"Marian put celery and water chestnuts in it. Makes it really crunchy."

"Delicious too. Is that apple?"

"Yep. Just a bit of Granny Smith. I watch her in the kitchen sometimes." She snags a napkin and wipes her chin. "Thinking maybe I'll learn through osmosis."

I swallow and give her a chuckle. "Well, this is amazing chicken salad."

"I'm glad you like it."

I continue eating, but then jerk when the doorbell rings.

CJ swallows her bite of sandwich and rises. "They have that big non-soliciting sign right out front, but it doesn't stop them. I swear I answer this door nine to ten times a day." She whisks away. "Be right back."

I finish my sandwich while she's gone and open my bag of chips.

I eat one, savoring the crunchiness and saltiness. Food tastes so good now. I mean, look at this potato chip. A thinly sliced piece of potato fried in oil and salted. That's all it is. And my God, it's delicious.

I finish the chips and drain my Diet Coke when I realize CJ hasn't come back yet.

I hear her talking at the door with someone, but I can't make out what either of them are saying.

I get up, walk out of the kitchen and toward the doorway, and then I gasp.

26

VINNIE

"Vinnie? What are you doing here?"

My gaze meets Raven Bellamy's.

I stop my jaw from dropping.

What the hell is she doing here in Giacomo Puzo's home?

Fuck. My job just got a lot more difficult.

Clarice widens her eyes. "You two know each other?"

"Yeah," Raven says. "He's my brother-in-law. Well, not really. My brother Falcon is engaged to his sister Savannah."

"Oh my God!" Clarice says. "Raven and I have known each other for years. We went to school together."

Really. Just kill me now.

Not only do I have to off the owner of this house, I have to off the employer of one of Raven's friends.

Fuck. It. All.

"So what are you doing here?" Raven asks again.

"I have some business with Mr. Puzo," I say.

Clarice looks back at Raven. "I keep telling him that Mr. Puzo is never home during the day."

"Which is why I came by, actually," I say. "I wanted to find out when he would be home. I was hoping to talk to Mrs. Puzo."

"Yeah, she doesn't check in with me, and she probably won't be home until dinnertime. But since you're a friend of Raven's and all, I guess you can hang out and wait if you want. In fact..."

Clarice looks at me and then at Raven and then back to me again. Her eyes widen slightly.

"Oh my God, Ray..." she says.

Raven gives her a punch in the arm. "Let it go," she says softly.

Let *what* go? What the hell is Raven talking about?

"All right," I say. "Thank you, Clarice."

Raven bursts into laughter. "Clarice? Since when do you go by Clarice?"

Clarice shrugs. "Since about five years ago. I decided it was a little more grown-up than CJ."

Raven cocks her head. "But you've always hated your name. Ever since Billy Doyle kept calling you Clarice and making that Hannibal Lecter sound in middle school."

"Yeah, well. I matured a little."

Raven chuckles. "Clarice Josephine Simons. I thought you'd be CJ forever."

"The name has kind of grown on me over the years. It's not like I got a cool bird name like you did. I was destined to be named after my great-grandmother."

"I think Clarice is a pretty name," I say.

I'm not sure why I said that. I don't really have any feelings one way or the other about the name. Now Raven, that's a beautiful name. A bird the same color as the peach fuzz on her head.

With piercing dark eyes.

Just like this woman's.

"The offer still stands," Clarice says. "You're welcome to stay here until Mrs. Puzo gets home. But like I said, it'll be probably around dinnertime."

"No." I look at my watch. "I don't have that much time. Got some other stuff to do. Would you please tell Mrs. Puzo to give me a call?"

"You mean she didn't call you last time?"

I shake my head. "Nope, she didn't."

She frowns. "I'll tell her again. Sorry about that."

"Not your fault. Good to see you again, Clarice. Raven." I nod.

Raven's cheeks are rosy pink. All I can think about is grabbing her and dragging her out to my car and having my way with her on the back seat.

Elmo might have a problem with that.

Then again, who the hell cares? He works for me.

Damn.

I'm still not used to this life.

Even though I grew up in it. Being second-in-command to the boss is...

Just fucking weird.

"Anyway, if you see Mr. Puzo—"

"I hardly ever see Mr. Puzo."

"Well, if you do, please give him my card and tell him I need to speak with him. It's urgent." I hand Clarice another card.

"I sure will."

I leave, and Clarice shuts the door behind her.

I walk to my car, get inside, and instruct Fred to take me to Grandfather's house.

"Right now," I say through gritted teeth.

"LISTEN, OLD MAN," I say to my grandfather, whose eyes widen at my words, "why in the hell did you tell me, when you wanted me to prove my loyalty, that I had to kill Raven Bellamy?"

Grandfather cocks his head. "I didn't."

"Don't give me that shit. Of course you did. And when I told you that would be personal, not business, you relented and gave me the name of Giacomo Puzo. Well, I've looked into Puzo. I went to his home today, hoping to find him. And guess who I found instead?"

"I couldn't begin to guess," Grandfather says.

"You think? Give it a try, Grandfather."

He simply stares at me. Glares at me, his watery eyes full of evil intent.

"Answer me," I say, making my voice as menacing as I can.

And damn, I'm good.

"It is no secret that I've had you watched. I am aware of course that you encountered Ms. Bellamy."

I nod coldly. "The *same* Ms. Bellamy that you ordered me to kill before turning your attention to Giacomo Puzo."

Grandfather's face remains as still as a statue. "So it would seem."

"So tell me." I cross the room and lean over his desk. "Is Giacomo Puzo actually an enemy of yours, or did you just tell me to kill him as an indirect means to get to Raven?"

A wicked laugh falls from my grandfather's lips. "Surely you don't believe that I, as connected as I am, would have the foresight to know that Puzo's nanny was an old college chum of hers."

"I believe you have the connections to be privy to all sorts of information you aren't entitled to." I point at him sharply. "And how did you know it was the nanny? I never told you that."

Grandfather steeples his fingers. "It was not difficult to ascertain. I know who is on Puzo's payroll. A simple social media search made it clear that the nanny went to the same school as Ms. Bellamy. Once I learned that she was present upon your second visit, it was easy to connect the dots. But if you are asking if I was aware of this connection before today, I'm afraid you're misguided."

I pace the office. There is no way in *hell* that this is a coincidence. I stop only to see my grandfather's eyes have widened, revealing two black holes of absolute iciness.

"And as for your first question, I wanted to see if you'd do it."

I scoff. "Man, you must really think I'm some evil son of a bitch. You honestly thought I would consider taking out an innocent young woman? A young woman who's already been through so much?"

"Everyone expected her to die," he says.

I shake my head. "You really are one motherfucking bastard."

He cackles then. Like an evil wizard laugh. "Vinnie, you have no idea."

I'm ready to quit now. Head back to Europe. Get the fuck out of here.

But I can't.

I made a commitment to protect Savannah. To protect my mother, who is the spawn of this evil bastard.

Maybe even get my father sprung from prison.

I can't do that from Europe.

"Puzo's nanny's friendship with your lady friend notwithstanding, he is still an enemy of this family," Grandfather continues. "What is your plan to take care of him?"

"It's in the works."

"Simply driving to his house and talking to his nanny or housekeeper is not in the works."

"Yeah, you gave me a gun to do it with. But don't you think you can trust me to do this my way?"

"I'm not sure I can trust you at all, Vincent. You left for seventeen years. You only came back for your sister."

"That's right. I came back for my sister. And my mother. Because they're my family."

He laughs again, shaking his head.

"The fuck is so funny about that?"

Grandfather crosses his hands over his chest in mock bashfulness. "I'm your family, Vincent. Don't I count?"

I roll my eyes. "After what you did to me? After what I'm pretty sure you did to Mikey? No, you don't. But Savannah and my mother and my father. They do. And the only way I can protect them is to do your bidding. So here I am, Grandpa. Take me as I am, or fucking get rid of me yourself."

He glares at me again.

And for a moment, I see an evil glint in his eyes. It's so evil that in that moment I'm convinced I just signed my own death certificate.

But a moment later he relaxes.

"You need to understand, Vincent, that what I did to you was just part of the process. I didn't do anything to you that wasn't done to me by my own father."

"And that's supposed to make it okay?"

"It was worse for me," he says. "My own father beat me up, beat me so my eyes were so swollen that I couldn't see. Then he took that billy club, and he did to me what I did to you. But he wasn't the only one. A few of his minions took their turns at me. But you know what? He didn't fucking break me."

"Did you hate him afterward?"

"For a while I did, until I learned to understand." He stands and paces behind his desk. "There's no room for weakness in this business. By the time they were all done with me, I was still on my two legs. It made me stronger. And I knew that I would one day wield the power they had over me. As you will one day wield over your own son."

"If you believe for one motherfucking *second* that I would ever do something like that to my own offspring, then you truly have another think coming." I cross behind his desk and poke him hard in his chest. "It didn't make me stronger. It just made me hate you. It made me want to get away from this family. So that's what I did. But I shouldn't have."

"You're right about that," Grandfather says.

"I shouldn't have because I should've been here to protect Mikey. I should've been here to protect my mother. Savannah. Even my father."

"Your father's weak."

"My father's one of the strongest men I know. He succeeded in keeping Savannah out of the McAllisters' clutches for years, and he protected Falcon for her at the cost of his freedom. And you know what? I would do the same thing for my own kid."

"You'd go to prison rather than work for me."

It's a statement, not a question. And we both know the truth of it.

I don't answer. I just keep staring him down. I'm convinced at some point he'll look away.

I've got to hand it to the old man. He's got more balls than any other octogenarian I've ever met.

But he doesn't know all the balls that I've got.

He doesn't know what happened to me in Europe. What I endured, and what I rose from.

No one knows.

And no one ever will.

27

RAVEN

To my surprise, CJ doesn't grill me about Vinnie. When she looked from me, to Vinnie, and then back to me again, I was certain she was putting two and two together.

She's already convinced I had sex, and when I looked at Vinnie, damn... Did I give away my secret?

I could feel how warm my cheeks were, how warm my chest was, how my legs wanted to give way beneath me.

But I held myself together.

Once he's gone, all CJ says is, "My God, he's hot, isn't he?"

"Very handsome," I say.

She smirks. "Handsome shmandsome. The man's a god." She looks at the card again. "Vincent Gallo Junior. Vincent Gallo. What a sexy name."

As if I needed reminding.

"It's been fun," I say. "But I should probably call my Uber. It'll be a long wait and—"

CJ shakes her head. "There's never a wait here."

"I thought you had a car to use?" I say.

"I do, but this is a burb. I have friends over from time to time who drink a little too much and need to call an Uber. You should be able to get one pretty fast."

"Still, it's a long drive." I grab my phone out of my pocket.

She grabs my arm. "Can't you stay a little longer? We haven't really gotten to talk much."

"Maybe for a little while." But then I look at my watch. "You know? I probably shouldn't. It's been so fun, Ceej, and you'll come to the ranch this weekend. Mom and Dad will be thrilled to see you too." I pull up the Uber app. Great, there's a ride five minutes away.

I give CJ a goodbye hug just as a Toyota Prius drives up to the house. "See you Sunday."

"Can't wait," CJ says.

I leave and hop into the car after checking the license plate. "Hi, I'm Raven. You're Johnson?"

"Yes, ma'am." He adjusts his phone on his hands-free car mount. "I see we've got a long ride ahead of us."

"Yeah. And if it's okay with you, I'm exhausted. I may just try to take a nap."

"Ma'am, that's fine with me."

I lean into the back seat and close my eyes.

I think about Vinnie Gallo.

And I wonder why he wants to see CJ's employers, the Puzos.

But I can't bring myself to care too much, because this is the most comfortable Prius I've ever been in. The seat seems to conform to my body, and I must fall asleep because in what seems like only about ten minutes, the car stops and Johnson says to me, "We're here, ma'am."

I shoot my eyes open. "Already?"

But before he answers, he gets out of the car and slides in the back seat next to me.

"What are you doing?" I ball my hands into fists. I didn't kick leukemia's ass just to be raped in the back of a car by an Uber driver.

"Nothing, ma'am. I just need to talk to you."

"About what? And if you touch me, I swear to God—" I put my hands up in front of my face.

"Calm down." He grabs my arms and forces them to my sides. "No one's going to hurt you."

"You already have. You've violated my rights." I reach into my pocket to grab my phone. "Uber will hear about this."

He knocks my phone out of my hands. "I'm pretty sure they won't give a shit since I'm not actually an Uber driver."

"Then how did you respond to my call?"

He grins. "Technology is easily hacked."

I let out a bloodcurdling scream.

He clamps his hand over my mouth. "Don't do that. It won't be good for either one of us."

I try to respond, but his hand over my mouth makes it impossible. I breathe heavily through my nose until he finally removes his hand.

"We good? You're not going to scream?"

I let out another bloodcurdling scream.

"Jesus fucking Christ." He clamps his hand over me again. "We're in an isolated area, and no one's going to hear you, ma'am. So please don't do that again."

For a criminal, he's being terribly polite. It's creepy.

He removes his hand slowly. "All I want to know is what you were doing at Giacomo Puzo's house."

"None of your business."

"We can do this the easy way or the hard way, ma'am. I don't want to hurt you." He forces his gaze onto mine. "But I will if I have to."

I don't yet have the physical strength to fight this man. There was a time, when I was younger and healthy, when I could kick ass nearly as well as my brothers and Robin. Unfortunately, that day is not today.

I swallow. "Fine. I was having lunch with a friend of mine. CJ Simons. She's their nanny."

He raises an eyebrow. "You sure that's all it was?"

"Why would it be anything else? I don't even know the Puzos."

"You know Vinnie Gallo?"

"Vinnie?" My nerves jolt all the way to my fingertips. "What do you want to know about Vinnie?"

Then I realize what this is about. I know what Vinnie's family does for a living. Somehow I got myself in the middle of it.

"His sister is engaged to my brother."

"Right. And I believe you were with him last night."

I say nothing. How the hell would he know? We were at my house. Nobody knows where my house is. I haven't even been living there.

"So what? He's a free agent, and so am I."

"Yes, he is. And you are as well. So I want you to do something for me."

He's kidding, right? He's basically abducted me and taken me to some unknown place when he was supposed to drive me home. This is false imprisonment, kidnapping, you name it.

Then again, he probably knows all of that.

"I hardly know the man," I say.

"I'd say you know him pretty well in the biblical sense." He narrows his eyes and looks me up and down. "I've got to say, for a bald chick you're pretty hot."

My hand absently wanders to my head. "Look, I hardly know him. We had some fun. Is that against the fucking law?"

"Not if you're both over eighteen, which I know he is." He trails his gaze down from my head to my breasts. "And I know you are."

"Exactly what else do you know about me?"

He shrugs. "Everything there is to know, Ms. Bellamy."

My skin tightens around my body, as if someone wrapped plastic wrap all over me. I feel violated. And not just because I've been kidnapped.

He says he knows everything about me, and already I know he's speaking the truth. He's said too many things that were accurate to truly be bullshitting me.

"If you really know who I am, you know my father's got money. A lot of money."

"I'm not interested in your money, Raven."

Raven now. Not Ms. Bellamy.

"What are you interested in?"

"Vinnie Gallo."

"I don't know what you need from me. You clearly know more about him than I do."

"True. But you can get close to him."

"Not if I choose not to. We had one night. It's not like we're in a relationship."

He cocks his head. "Would you like to be?"

His question stuns me. Because the answer on the tip of

my tongue is yes, I would like to be in a relationship with Vinnie Gallo. But I know what he does for a living. And I know he's got his work cut out for him if he wants to bring down his family.

And he said he couldn't go any further with me and had no intention of doing so. He damn near broke my heart, but I'm not telling this asshole any of that.

"To be honest, I haven't given it a lot of thought," I lie.

He leans in, his teeth gritted. "Then get good at pretending. I need you to give him a call. Set a date for, say, this Friday evening."

"That's two days from now," I say, "and I already have another date."

His eyebrows nearly fly off his head. "Really? Is baldness *in* now or something?"

I close my eyes, count to ten. I really want to scream again. More than that, I want to claw this guy's eyes out, but my fingernails are short right now.

I need Robin here. She may have been a tomboy when we were growing up, but she wears her nails long and lethal.

I decide not to dignify his comment with a response.

"Like I said…I'm busy." He doesn't need to know that I was going to cancel the date with Brick anyway.

"Cancel it," he says again.

"No," I say succinctly.

"I'll make it worth your while if you cancel it."

I scoff. "What could you possibly do to make it worth my while? I come from money. I'm recovering from leukemia. I almost died. So unless you can guarantee me that I'll be leukemia-free—make that free from cancer and any other catastrophic illness—for the rest of my life, I'm not interested."

He turns his gaze away from me then, looks toward the front of the car.

Right. He says he knows everything about me, but he hasn't given me a lot of thought. Hasn't put anything into my perspective. When you're ill—when you feel like you'd rather die than go through one more day of the pain—you realize that money and material things really mean nothing.

Don't get me wrong. I'm glad I have them. Money does make life a lot easier. But I would've given it all up in a heartbeat to be free from that devastating illness.

"I can guarantee you that your brothers will live."

My jaw drops. "Leave my brothers out of this."

"I'll be happy to..." He leans in again, poking me in the upper chest with every word he speaks. "If you break the date with whoever you're going out with and see Vinnie Friday night instead."

That's hardly a hardship, which is why I know it can't be that easy.

"And?" I ask.

"And...your instructions will come." He pulls a burner phone out of his pocket and hands it to me. "You'll get a text. All you have to do now is call Vinnie and make a date for Friday night."

"I'm not going to hurt Vinnie."

"Who asked you to?"

"*You're* asking me to." I push at his chest with my hands. "You think I'm so naïve as to think you just want me to go out on a date with Vinnie Gallo Friday night?"

This guy clearly has no idea that Vinnie has no intention of seeing me again. He'll say no.

"All you need to do is call him," Johnson says. "Ask him to meet you at your place. Cook him a nice dinner. And make sure he doesn't leave until after midnight."

28

VINNIE

I actually get home in time for dinner.

"Hey, Mom," I call.

"Vincent, darling." My mom walks toward me swiftly and gives me a hug. "It's so great to see you here. Luisa made one of her Italian feasts. I know how much you love Italian."

The aroma is absolutely tantalizing, yet it does nothing for me. "I'm not too hungry, Mom."

She furrows her brow. "You have to eat. You need to keep your strength. And tomorrow…"

"What about tomorrow?"

"Don't you remember? It's visitors' day. We're going to see your father in prison."

I draw a breath. Shit. I forgot. "Sure, Mom. When do you want to leave?"

"First thing in the morning. We can see him as early as nine o'clock."

"All right. I'll have to call Grandfather and tell him I won't be in."

She casts her gaze to the floor. "I hate that man."

All I can do is nod.

We both know how I feel about him. My mother doesn't know everything he put me through before I left the country. She'll never know. I can't do that to her.

"I hate that you have to do this, Vinnie," she says. "If Savannah had just done her duty and married that McAllister boy—"

I hold up my hand to stop my mother. "You mean the guy who tried to rape her? Give it a rest, Mom. I'm home, and I'm glad to be home. But I won't have you talking about Savannah that way. She's with the man she loves, and she deserves that much."

She crosses her arms. "Your father's in prison because of her."

"Dad's in prison by his own decision. I would've done the same thing if it had come to that. Doesn't someone in this family deserve to be happy?"

My mother sighs. "I know I sound punitive. I do love your sister." She gazes out the window into our backyard. "She was my little girl. And I let her have a childhood. I let her have an amazing childhood until we were forced to move here to Austin right before her senior year of high school. She had to leave all of her friends in Long Island, and she was the new girl at school. I don't think she ever got over that." She turns to me. "Your father coddled her, Vinnie. He let her off the hook at eighteen, and then again at twenty-two. And then again... When she wanted to leave her job as a parole officer here in Austin. Your father let her go."

"Except that he didn't."

She looks down. "There were...extenuating circumstances."

I lift my eyebrows at my mother. "How would you know that? Dad and Grandpa haven't told you anything, have they?"

"I just know the way things are, Vinnie." She leans on the counter. "I was born into this life and I've lived it for all of my fifty-four years. Your father had a soft spot for Savannah. He would've never gone back on his promise and tried to force her into that marriage if his hands hadn't been tied."

I draw in another breath. I'm pretty sure my mother is speaking the truth. What was it that drove Grandfather to the point where he decided to expand the business beyond drugs?

Something's going on that I don't know about, and I intend to find out everything.

But the first thing I need to do is find a friend. A friend in law enforcement—local, state, and federal.

Because I'm going to do something that I'm going to need immunity for.

I open my mouth to say something when my phone buzzes with a text.

I pull it out of my pants pocket and take a look. It's Raven.

Call me when you get the chance.

Raven? She wouldn't text me unless it was something important. My God... Is she still at the Puzos' place?

"Excuse me for a minute, Mom."

She nods and heads back to the kitchen. "Come join me for dinner when you're ready."

I nod back at her and then punch Raven's number into my phone, bringing it to my ear.

"Hello?" Her voice shakes a little.

Maybe it's just my imagination.

"Raven, it's Vinnie. I just got your text."

She clears her throat. "Oh, good. It was nice to see you today."

"Great to see you too."

"I was wondering... I don't mean to be forward or anything, but would you like to come to my place for dinner Friday evening?"

My heart skips a beat. "So you canceled your date?"

"Yeah, I did. I think I'd much rather spend the evening with you."

Her voice sounds off. I made it pretty clear that what happened between us couldn't happen again. Of course, the tightness in my groin proves my cock didn't get that message. But Raven got it, and she's not an unreasonable person. Why is she asking me to dinner then?

And why do I want to go more than I want to breathe? Something's not right here.

"Sure, Raven. I'd be happy to come."

"Great." Although the tone of her voice doesn't sound like it's great.

"What time?" I ask.

She pauses. "How about around six thirty? Do you remember the way to my place?"

Seriously? It's seared into my memory. "Yeah, I do. I'll see you then, Raven."

"Great." Again she doesn't sound like it's great. She clears her throat again. "See you then, Vinnie."

I end the call and shove my phone back in my pocket. Why did she sound so strange?

I can check in with Falcon later. See if he knows anything. Otherwise, I'll see her Friday night for our date.

I'm glad she decided to break the date with the lawyer. I have to say I'm surprised that she asked me out. She doesn't seem the forward type that way.

Then again… I hardly know her.

As I ENTER my grandfather's office the next morning, a question arises in my mind.

How many lives has he taken?

I'm sure he is responsible for the ending of many lives, but I want to know how many he personally has taken.

It's not my place to ask.

My only place is to prove my loyalty to him and the family. And to do that, I have to get rid of Puzo.

What my grandfather doesn't know is that I have already taken a life.

And if I found myself in the same circumstances? I would do it again.

But I can't get used to it. The problem with things you're not supposed to do is that once you do them, it's easier to do them again. You continue and you continue, and if you get away with it, you feel a little less guilt with each time you do it.

How do I take a man's life?

I've already determined that Puzo is hardly a pillar of society. The world will be a better place without him. Hell, the world would be a hell of a better place without my grandfather in it.

If only I could off him and get it over with.

But it's not that simple.

There are people in this organization who are loyal to my grandfather. Not to me yet.

But I will prove myself.

And his will be the last life I take.

My grandfather clears his throat. "I'm getting tired of waiting, Vincent."

"You want me to be careless about it? If so, I'll get it done this afternoon."

"You've been to his house twice."

"Yeah, and he's out of town." I take a seat across from him. "And by the way, I don't appreciate you watching me."

"How else am I supposed to be sure of your loyalty? Your trust?"

"By not watching me," I say. "I'm not a fucking kid, Grandfather. I'm no longer eighteen. I don't need a babysitter."

"Seems you may. Puzo is still among the living."

I open my mouth to say something, but he holds up a hand.

"I'm sick and tired of your excuses, Vinnie. You get it done today, or someone you care about may meet the same fate."

He's not talking about Savannah. She's his little cricket. And he's certainly not talking about his daughter, my mother.

He could be talking about Falcon. Or my father.

But my guess is that he's talking about Raven Bellamy.

"I've got to go," I say. "My mother and I are going to see my father in prison this morning."

"You want to waste your time with that?"

"He's your son-in-law. Your daughter's husband. And he's

my father. So yes, I'm going to go see him, and I don't consider it a waste of time."

"You've got until midnight tomorrow night, Vinnie." He stands slowly, leering over the desk. "I want Puzo's head on a platter by then, or you will be sorry."

His words send a chill through me.

I don't doubt their veracity. My grandfather is evil incarnate. Fucking Lucifer himself.

And he doesn't make threats idly.

I rise without saying another word, walk out of his office, and then drive the few miles to pick up Mom.

She's waiting for me.

Her hands are on her hips. "Vinnie, where'd you go this morning?"

"I had to go see Grandfather. To tell him where I was going today."

"You couldn't have just given him a call?"

For being the daughter of this man, my mother doesn't know him at all. No, I couldn't just give him a call. He expects to see me first thing in the morning in his office every day. It's something I agreed to.

"I'm afraid it doesn't work that way, Mom. Come on."

I gave my driver a few hours off. I'm driving us to the prison myself. Of course, I know we'll be followed. Grandfather's watching my every move. But I feel this is something Mom and I need to do on our own.

It'll be our first visitation with him since he got incarcerated. He pleaded guilty to the murder of Miles McAllister, and he's in for life.

Of course, in our family, life means "until Grandfather is no longer pissed off at you."

Mom and I don't speak much during the drive, and when I pull into the prison parking lot, a heavy silence hangs in the car. The towering walls of the prison loom over us, ominous and foreboding. I glance at my mother. Her eyes are closed, her hands clasped tightly in her lap. She takes a deep breath, turning toward me with a hollow smile.

"Let's get this over with," she says, unbuckling her seatbelt.

We walk in silence on the concrete pavement. When we arrive, we're taken through several gates and checkpoints where guards give us scrutinizing stares before ushering us forward. Finally, we're led into a room filled with more guards, inmates, and their families. The room buzzes with hushed whispers.

My father sits at one of the tables, looking older and more haggard than I remember him. He's in a faded orange jumpsuit, and his elbows are on the table, his hands supporting his head. When he sees us, his eyes light up, but even the minute amount of joy seeing us has granted him can't extinguish the sadness dominating them.

"Vinnie," he says, standing to hug me. His grip is firm, a stark contrast to the frailty I see in his features.

He turns to Mom and takes her shaking hands in his. She can't bring herself to look at him. She just nods, tears streaming down her face.

"We're here for you," I tell him, voice steady despite the lump forming in my throat.

Dad takes a seat. "Where's Savannah?"

Mom frowns. "She couldn't get away. Something with Falcon's parents, I guess."

"She's devastated she couldn't make it, Dad, but she'll make the next visit," I say.

Dad nods sadly. "Of course. I know you can't all rearrange your lives around me."

Mom reaches forward and grabs his hand. "How are you doing here, sweetheart?"

Dad shakes his head. "I don't want to talk about my life here. I want to know how you are doing." He turns to me. "Is your grandfather treating you all right?"

I shrug. "He's treating me as well as he is capable of doing, I guess."

Dad then gives me an inquisitive look, as if he's tacitly trying to ask if my grandfather has given me any grisly assignments. I give him a curt nod, making sure Mom is looking away when I do. Dad's eyes get even sadder, but he reassumes his poker face quickly when Mom looks back.

"It's just wonderful to see you both." He looks at Mom. "How are things going in the home, honey?"

Mom sighs. "It's not the same without you, of course. But it is wonderful to have Vinnie with us again." Her face twists and she reaches into her bag for a tissue. "Of course, my dream would be to have all three of my men together again. You, Vinnie, and little Mikey." She dabs at her eyes. "But that of course can never happen."

Dad reaches forward, grabs her free hand. "You might get two out of three."

"You're in for life, Vincent."

"You know just as well as I do that I'm only in here as long as your esteemed father deems necessary for me to learn my lesson."

Mom blows her nose in the tissue. "That bastard will never let you out."

Dad and I both widen our eyes. It's not like Mom to use profanity, especially not about her own flesh and blood. Nobody speaks for a few endless minutes. Finally I decide to break the silence.

I uneasily pat my mother on the shoulder. "You never know, Mom. I'm doing my best to earn Grandfather's trust, and once I have it, I think I'll be able to use my influence to get him to help Dad get out of here."

Mom buries her face in her hands. "I never wanted this for any of my children."

"We saved Savannah, Mom. Who's to say we can't save the rest of you?"

Mom looks up. "But what about *you*, Vinnie? I can't allow you to take the fall for me or for your father."

"No good parent would," Dad agrees.

"Well, as it stands, I'm the only one who *can*. So I will." I look at the clock. "We're running out of time. Dad, is there anything else you wanted to catch up on?"

We chat inanely about nothing in particular for the remaining time allotted for visitors. But that's okay. It's nice to just spend some time with my father.

As our hour comes to an end, Mom excuses herself to go to the ladies' room. Dad pulls me aside. His expression is somber, his eyes bearing into mine. "Vinnie," he starts, his voice a mere whisper, "I know what your grandfather wants you to do. Don't let him push you into this. You're better than that."

I look away, the cold hardness of the prison walls mirroring the hardened resolve building within me. "Well,

Dad," I murmur, "if I don't do it, he'll never trust me enough to give me the reins."

"You don't have to be part of this life," he says. "I didn't want this for you. I didn't want you to carry these burdens." His words hang heavy in the air between us.

"Being part of this family *means* carrying burdens," I reply, my voice hoarse. "You know that better than anyone."

Before he can argue further, a stern voice announces the end of visitation hours. I hug my father one last time, his whispered warnings still echoing in my ears. Mom returns, and they embrace. This time she meets his gaze.

"I love you, Caroline," he says.

"I love you too, Vince. So much."

The ride home is even quieter than the ride there. I glance at my mother as we pull into the driveway. She's staring out of the window with a glazed look in her eyes. Neither of us says a word as we make our way into the house.

Soon after, I find myself alone in Dad's study, nursing a glass of whiskey. I swirl it around in the glass, watching as it clings to the sides before sliding back down.

My father's words replay in my mind. *"You're better than that."*

Am I really? Or am I just deluding myself? This is the life we were born into, the world we inherited. Burdens and bloodshed, secrets and threats—they're in our veins, under our skin. We can't escape it any more than a wolf can escape its hunger.

As I take another sip of the whiskey, I look upward and stare at the spinning blades of the ceiling fan. They whirl around in an endless cycle, like our family caught in an unending loop of violence and power struggles. My grandfather's ultimatum echoes in my mind: Puzo's head on a platter by midnight tomorrow or else somebody I care about will meet their end.

Raven Bellamy.

The thought of her caught up in this makes my gut churn with dread. I empty the glass and pour myself another, trying to drown out my fears with alcohol. But it doesn't help. Nothing helps when you're living on borrowed time.

Time's up.

Raven Bellamy shouldn't be tangled up in this mess, our family mess, but she is. Because of me.

I'm the reason she's in danger, and I will be the one to ensure she gets out unscathed, whatever the cost.

My phone buzzes on the desk, snapping me out of my thoughts. It's a text message from an unknown number with a single sentence.

She's safe. For now.

Fear lances sharply through me, its icy grip squeezing my heart. She isn't safe, not as long as she's associated with me. I toss the phone onto my bed. How did it come to this? My vicious grandfather, my father rotting away behind bars, and now Raven—sweet, innocent Raven—caught in the crossfire of our familial warfare.

And what of the date with her tomorrow night?

I won't break it. If I'm with her, I can protect her.

So I need to take care of Puzo before then.

I swiftly type a reply.

I'll do what needs to be done.

29

RAVEN

I wake up with my teeth chattering.

Once the faux Uber driver was done talking to me, he brought me home, safe and sound.

But I don't feel safe and sound.

I desperately wanted to call Vinnie last night. But I had been forced to call him by the Uber driver and I didn't want to bother him again.

He agreed to meet me at my place tomorrow evening, and that's all that matters. I'm supposed to get further instructions via the burner phone that feels like it's literally burning a hole into me.

But tomorrow evening I'll level with Vinnie. I'll tell him what happened.

He'll fix it. I know Vinnie will be able to fix it.

I have to get a grip. I could go to my mother and father. They would help me. But that might put Vinnie in danger. And Vinnie is Savannah's brother, so it may put Falcon in danger as well.

I don't want anyone to be in danger because of me.

Damn it!

Why? Why did I have to go and fall in love with—

No.

I'm not in love with him.

He's a mobster. A gangster. And even though I know in his heart he's a good man who only wants to bring his evil grandfather down, danger will follow him.

Which means danger will follow me.

Why do I need to have him over to my place for dinner? What is the purpose behind it, and who is that damned Uber driver?

How did they hack into my Uber request?

Chills erupt over my body. I look at my clock. It's nine in the morning. My mother won't bother me. She probably looked in the room a couple times throughout the night to make sure I'm all right. She doesn't know that I've actually been up most of the night, my mind racing.

I draw a breath. Let it out slowly. Draw in another. I try to calm my shivers. Despite the fact that it's a warm day in Texas—and warm in Texas means infernally hot—I'm still shivering.

I've got to get this under control before I go to the kitchen.

I take several more deep breaths. I try to focus on something good, something happy.

I'm alive! The leukemia didn't kill me! At this point, it's likely that I'm going to have a normal lifespan.

One more deep breath and then I rise.

I shower, rubbing the loofah over my head and over the rest of my body.

When I get out of the shower, I look in the mirror.

My hair is growing in enough that it's difficult to see my

scalp at this point. In several more weeks, I'll have a cute pixie cut.

My cheeks are red from the heat of the shower, and I decide I look okay.

I get dressed quickly in some denim shorts and a tank top, no bra.

Everything else seems to be too much effort.

How am I going to get to my place tomorrow? How will I explain to Mom that I need to go there?

I grab my phone and put a call in to my doctor's office.

"Lone Star Wellness," the receptionist says.

"Yes, hi. Good morning." I clear my throat to stop my voice from cracking. "This is Raven Bellamy. I'm a patient of Dr. Smith's. I was wondering if he was available?"

"I believe he just finished with a patient. I may be able to catch him. Please hold for a moment."

"Sure. Thank you."

A moment later, "Raven? It's Dr. Smith."

"Yes, Doctor. I just wanted to check in with you and see if you could clear me for driving."

"I think you've got another week to go." He pauses a moment, probably checking my chart. "But let me ask you this. How are you feeling?"

"I'm feeling great. I'm eating well."

"No fogginess? Dizziness?"

"Not at all. I was just wondering if maybe you could clear me to drive short distances? No longer than like fifteen minutes to half an hour behind the wheel?"

He pauses again. "You've responded very well to treatment. I suppose it's all right. If you're feeling okay."

"Oh yes, Doctor. I'm feeling just fine. I just want to get back to normal, you know? It seems like it's been so long."

"I totally understand. Tell you what. I will clear you to drive, but I don't want you behind the wheel for any longer than about twenty minutes. Is that all right?"

"That's perfect. Thanks."

"But you let me know if anything happens. And if at any time you do not feel comfortable behind the wheel, you pull over, you call for a ride. Is that clear?"

"Crystal. Don't worry. I'm not going to do anything to jeopardize my recovery."

"I know you won't, Raven. You've been through hell, and it's time for you to get back among the living. I totally understand. I've marked your chart."

"Thank you so much, Dr. Smith. I promise everything will be fine."

"I know it will be. Have a good day, Raven."

I end the call, and I repeat the words I just said to Dr. Smith in my head.

I promise everything will be fine.

As far as my recovery goes? As far as driving goes?

My words are true. I feel it in the marrow of my bones.

Everything else, though?

That's up in the air.

I head downstairs. Mom is still in the kitchen. "Raven, there you are. Breakfast?"

My stomach is a void, and I feel like if I eat anything I'll throw it back up. Still, I need to think of my body. Of sustenance. What it needs.

"Just two scrambled eggs and toast please."

Mom wrinkles her nose. "That's exactly what you had for breakfast yesterday. Are you feeling all right?"

"Yeah, I feel fine. Just want something easy to digest. Thanks, Mom."

"Coming right up." She smiles. "You look good today, Raven."

I stop my eyebrows—or lack thereof—from flying off my forehead. I look good? I feel...physically okay, I guess. I'm stressed as all hell.

"That's because I have some great news." I make my voice deliberately sing-songy to feign happiness.

"What's that?"

"I just talked to Dr. Smith, and he cleared me for driving."

She furrows her brow. "I thought you had another week to go."

"I just really want to get back to normal, so I called him. And he said as long as I haven't had any dizziness or fogginess, it would be okay for me to drive short distances. So this way I can go to my house. Get things fixed up for when I move home in a few weeks."

"Raven..."

"Call Dr. Smith if you don't believe me. I just talked to him."

"Oh no, I believe you." She wraps her arms around me, stroking the small amount of hair I have on my head. "I'm just worried. It's a mother's prerogative, you know."

I smile, forcing myself to look happy again. Keeping my voice upbeat. "I know you do. But I want to enjoy life again. I want to go to my house. Do you know how long it's been since I've been there?"

Only two days, but she doesn't know that.

"I understand, dear. Truly I do." She breaks the embrace and looks into my eyes. "Would you do me a favor?"

"Of course."

"Call me when you get to your house, so I know you're okay?"

"Absolutely, I will. But I may also need to go into town and get some groceries."

"Groceries?"

"Yeah. You know. So I can make myself a sandwich or something while I'm hanging out there and fixing stuff up."

"All right, Raven. But do your mama a favor. Just let me know you're okay. Text me every hour."

"Every hour?"

She sighs. "All right. Just text me when you're there safely."

"I may not be home for dinner tomorrow," I say.

"You won't?"

"Well, you know. I have a date. With my lawyer, Brick Latham."

Which reminds me. I still need to cancel that.

"Oh, that's great. You sure you're ready for that?"

"He must think I am because he asked me out. I'll just have him pick me up at my place. Most of my clothes are still there anyway.'

She opens her mouth—

I hold up a hand to stop her. "And yes, I will call you when we leave on the date, and I will call you when I get home safely."

"Will you be coming back here for the night?"

"Yes, probably. But it may be late."

"All right, Raven." She sighs. "I knew I wouldn't be able to keep you here forever. But I did get used to having my baby girl around." She wraps her arms over my shoulders. "If you ever have kids, you'll know what I mean."

"Thanks, Mom. I love you. Maybe you and Dad can go out tonight. Catch a movie, some dinner. Something fun." I frown. "You haven't gotten to do *anything* fun in so long."

Mom smiles. "Maybe we'll do just that, angel." She kisses me on top of my head and then looks into my eyes. Creases of worry snake across her forehead.

I can see that she's not comfortable with this. Honestly, I'm not good with it either. I'm lying to my mother, and I hate that.

But I feel like I have no choice.

I don't regret meeting Vinnie, sleeping with Vinnie.

It was the most amazing experience of my life.

Right now, though? I'm frightened.

Frightened for him. And for me.

30

VINNIE

Grandfather's words ring in my mind.

You have until midnight tomorrow night.

Rather tonight, at this point.

Raven's call two days ago surprised me. I want to have dinner with her at her place. I'd love to take her to bed again.

I'm happy about it.

Happy to be seeing Raven, of course.

But it also gives me an alibi.

Giacomo Puzo will die tonight while I'm at Raven's.

No one will suspect me.

Not that it matters anyway. It gave me a way to set it in motion.

I found out where he is.

He's in Houston on business.

So I'm driving there now. I'll put into motion my plan to take care of things.

Just as my grandfather took credit for Diego Vega when I know he had nothing to do with his death, I will take credit for Puzo.

After all, what's good for the goose is good for the gander. I spent all day yesterday putting everything together. I remembered seeing in his medical records that he's deathly allergic to peanuts, and I've arranged for his dinner to be laced with peanut butter. I paid off a maid to abscond with his epi-pen.

Easy enough.

He's toast.

Do I feel remorse? A bit. I don't know the man personally, but I know he's a two-bit mobster who's gotten involved with some Colombian thugs.

Arivaderci, Giacomo.

I REACH Raven's house at six o'clock. Again, I'm traveling without my driver.

Having a driver feels all wrong to me.

I hate every part of this life. And frankly? I don't want anyone knowing where I am tonight.

Which is why I rented a car with cash and a fake ID.

I remember a few secrets from my youth.

Who to call to get a fake ID is one of them, and to my surprise it's even easier now with technology. I had to jump through many hoops to get my papers to leave the country and I forged many more documents while I was abroad. Today? It was easy.

Perhaps I'm still being followed. I don't know.

But I do know there's no tracer on this rental. There is one on my Mercedes, no doubt showing my grandfather everywhere I go. It wasn't difficult to find it, and I left it there. Let him think he's controlling me. At the moment, my car is at my parents' house.

The car I rented is a beige Ford. Non-descript. It's perfect. It's tiny, and my long legs are cramped in the driver's seat, but I don't care.

If I could get the hell out of here—and take Raven with me—I'd be happy to drive this car for the rest of my life.

I'd be happy to live in a hut in the hills.

But that's not my destiny.

My destiny is to take down my grandfather and destroy the legacy of our family.

I will do it.

I get out of the car and go to the door, knocking lightly. Raven opens the door with a smile on her face.

Only…something is wrong with her smile. Normally when she smiles, her eyes crinkle really adorably, and a tiny amount of blood rushes to her cheeks, making them glow. Right now, her eyes are a little distant, and her face is pale. It doesn't seem…real.

I haven't known this woman long, but already I feel like I can read her. Something's bothering her.

Maybe I'm wrong though. She *is* recovering from cancer. Even though she's well on the road to recovery, she might just be a little more spent than normal today. Hopefully not *too* spent, because I have been looking forward to dinner—and maybe even a little dessert—with her since she called and arranged our date.

"Hi, Vinnie. I'm so glad you could make it."

I walk through the door, give her a kiss on the cheek. "You okay?"

And then, to my surprise, Raven bursts into tears.

I guess she's *really* had a bad day.

I go to her, take her in my arms. Kiss her head, her cheeks, her neck. "Raven, baby. What is it?"

"Do you think we can speak freely here?" she asks.

I drop my jaw and pull back from her. "What's going on, Raven?"

"I shouldn't tell you this. But when I was at CJ's the other day, I called an Uber to drive me home. At some point I must have dozed off, and when I woke up, the driver had pulled over to the side of the road—"

I go rigid.

What did this driver do to her? Did he hurt her? Force himself on her?

I can't help but wonder if my grandfather is behind this. He's always trying to assert himself over me. And he knows who my Achilles heel is.

But we shouldn't talk about this here. Raven is right to be concerned. No one has lived here for the past several years, and my grandfather *did* know where I was the other night.

Anyone could've come in and put in surveillance equipment. And nobody would've been the wiser.

"Jesus fuck."

"He didn't hurt me, Vinnie. I swear."

"Are you sure? If there is one mark on you..." I look around her house. I didn't pay much attention the other night as I couldn't wait to get her into bed. Then I left so quickly and took her home.

If the house is bugged...

"Do you have a security system here?" I ask.

She shakes her head. "No. I was going to get one, and then I got sick."

"When was the last time you were here? The other night? With me?"

"No. I was here yesterday cleaning up. My doctor gave me the okay to drive, and then I came over today and got groceries, and—"

I place my fingers over my lips to quiet her. "Let's go outside."

She nods and leads me through the foyer to the kitchen and out the French doors. We walk off the large redwood deck and into the grassy area behind her house. The pool house and swimming pool are off to the right, and an alcove with a gazebo sits to the left.

She leads me there and we sit down.

"Tell me everything. Did he hurt you? Is there a mark anywhere on you?" My heart is racing, and my hands are balled into fists.

"No, there isn't. I swear to God, Vinnie. I'm unharmed. Other than the fact that he scared the hell out of me."

"Did he have a weapon?"

"Not that I saw."

"Where did you stop?"

"On one of the back roads between Austin and Summer Creek. I suppose I could've gotten out of the car and run, but where would I have gone?"

I grab her arm a bit more forcefully than I intend. But I don't let go. "Tell me what happened, Raven. Every single detail. That motherfucker will pay."

She looks around, gulping back a sob. "I'll ask you again. Do you think we can speak freely here?"

I take her in my arms again, embrace her, kiss her lips.

I look above the gazebo. It's unlikely there's surveillance, but how the hell should I know? I take her hand and we walk out into the yard, the Texas sun beginning its descent in the west.

"Talk now," I say, cupping her cheek. "We should be safe here."

She gulps. "He just said that I needed to call you and ask you to dinner tonight. Then he gave me this burner phone." She pulls it out of her back pocket and hands it to me. "He said to get you here, and then I'd get further instructions. But nothing has come. At least not yet." She points to a few lawn chairs sitting around a fire pit in the distance. "I need to sit down."

We walk toward the chairs and sit down next to each other.

"I just need you to know," she says, sniffling. "I heard what you said the other night. That it can't happen again with us. The call for tonight. It wasn't about that. It was because he made me call you and—" She gasps.

"What?" My heart thumps. "What is it, Raven?"

"I... I forgot to cancel the date with Brick. He's probably showing up at my house right about now. How could I be so stupid?"

"Your mom can send him away."

She shakes her head. "No, I didn't tell her I was going to break the date. She would just send him here." She runs her hands over her scalp. "Except Mom said she might take Dad out for the evening. So he'll just arrive to an empty house. God, he'll think I'm such a bitch!"

I take her hand, rubbing my thumb into her palm. "Do you have your phone on you?"

She nods.

"Text him now. Quickly. Then that's one thing off your plate. Tell him you lost track of time and… I don't know. Just make something up."

She pulls out her cellphone and taps lightly. "Done," she says.

"Okay. That's one less thing to worry about." I attempt a smile. "Did he say anything else?"

"No. But he hacked my Uber app. That's how he got to me. When I called an Uber to take me home from CJ's. Or the Puzos'. Whatever."

The Puzos. Fuck it all. How is this all related?

"We need to get out of here," I tell her.

"What?"

"We need… Whoever called you knows where we both are tonight. It's not safe here, Raven."

A look of determination takes over her fine features. "This is my home, damn it. I made you dinner. Spaghetti with marinara sauce. And I grabbed a baguette from the local bakery."

"I'm sure it's delicious. We can wrap it up and take it with us."

But her eyes say something else. She won't be chased out of her own home.

Damn. I could so easily fall for her beauty, her strength, her integrity.

Then she jerks in her chair. "What's that?"

"What's what?"

"Some kind of buzzing sound. Don't you hear it?"

I concentrate, and yes…I hear it. "It sounds like a dragonfly or something."

But it's no dragonfly.

"Stay here," I tell her.

"I'm going with you, wherever you're going," she says adamantly.

I put my fingers to my lips again and look toward the noise.

A drone floats above us about twenty-five feet in the air.

Raven throws a hand over her mouth. "My God!"

I point to the house. "Go back toward the house. I'll take care of it."

She nods and walks briskly away. I take out my phone and text my grandfather.

Get out of here or I'm done.

I wait for a response. Five minutes. Six agonizing minutes. Seven. Eight...

The drone finally flies away.

"Motherfucker," I say under my breath.

A cheap rental car and a fake ID isn't enough to throw Mario Bianchi off track. I didn't for a minute think they would be.

It should be enough to throw Puzo's goons off track though.

Because right about now?

Puzo ought to be good and dead.

31

RAVEN

I rub my arms against the chill. "Was that really a drone?" I ask Vinnie when he returns from the chairs.

"It was. But you don't have to worry about it. I had it called off. Let's just go have dinner."

"Can we talk in there?"

"It's probably better if we don't."

I swallow. So he thinks my house is bugged. "Okay. I'll get our dinner ready. We can eat. And then we can..."

"Fuck the food, Raven. I think we both need a little escape right now." He holds out his hand to me.

I take it, and together we walk back into the house, saying nothing, and we go straight to my bedroom.

I can feel him studying me, his dark gaze searching my face. There's an urgency in his grip, a desperation that wasn't there before. I can't help but lose myself in the connection, my nerves on fire from his touch.

We reach the bedroom and he releases my hand to shut the door behind us. Vinnie moves to the window and peeks through the blinds.

Then he turns to me.

"I want you," he growls.

Despite my fear and nerves—and the knowledge that someone could be watching and listening—my body responds to his words. "I want you too."

He steps toward me, raking his fingers through his hair. "You don't understand," he says. "It's not just physical."

I drop my jaw, a flood of emotions crashing over me. His confession makes my heart nearly stop. "Then what is it?"

Vinnie moves forward, planting his hands on either side of me against the wall, his body so close to mine that I can feel his breath on my face. His eyes hold mine prisoner. The intensity makes me shiver.

"Every day," he begins in a hushed whisper, "every single day since I've met you, I wake up with your name on my lips. You're the last thought in my mind before I sleep. You've become an obsession, Raven."

A gasp escapes from me and I can feel every muscle in his body tense. Heat is coming off him in waves.

"I shouldn't drag you into this. I had no intention of doing it, but I seem powerless to stop it."

I hold up my hand. "I know what you're up against, Vinnie," I say. "I know you want to bring down your family. I know it's dangerous. But I'm not afraid of danger. I nearly died from the cancer. This is my second chance, Vinnie, and I want you to be a part of it."

Vinnie's eyebrows crease, the tension emanating from him as palpable as the heat between our bodies. "Raven," he murmurs, "you don't understand. It's more than taking out one person. It's a dark alley with no end."

"I'm not afraid of the dark," I say. "I've been there before, remember? I fought my way back once, and I can do it again. But this time, I won't be alone, because you'll be there."

He rests his hands on my shoulders, gripping them gently. He heaves a sigh as he drops his forehead to mine.

"You're absolutely amazing," he murmurs against my skin. I can hear the smile in his voice. "I should stay away. And I'm an idiot for allowing myself to fall for you."

My heart stands still. Did he just admit he's in love with me?

"I... I guess we make quite the pair then."

Vinnie chuckles, a soft rumbling sound that vibrates against me. "Yeah," he says, his voice laced with an emotion that sounds disturbingly like defeat. "I guess we do."

We stay silent for a long while, our breaths the only noise in the room. The thoughts whirl around my head like a tornado, but the feeling of Vinnie's body against mine brings a sense of calm that I have no business feeling given the circumstances we find ourselves in.

But before I can dwell further on these thoughts, he pulls back slightly, just enough to look at me. His eyes are serious.

"Raven," he says firmly, "Promise me something."

"Anything."

"Promise me that you'll remember who you are—that you'll remember this feeling—no matter what happens next."

A pit forms in my stomach. His words echo of some foreboding doom. I swallow and nod. "I promise, Vinnie. I won't forget."

"Good," he murmurs, wrapping me in his arms once more, holding me so close that it feels like we're one person. "And remember this too—I love you."

The words hit me like a physical blow, stealing my breath.

A lump forms in my throat as tears prick the corners of my eyes.

He said he couldn't do this. That we couldn't... That it would never be...

But all I hear are his words.

I love you.

"I love you too," I whisper, reaching up to kiss him.

No truer words. How did it happen? I don't know. I don't care. All I know is that I love Vinnie, and nothing else matters. Not the drone following us. Not the Uber driver. Not Vinnie's grandfather. Not the body buried on the Bellamy ranch.

Nothing.

Nothing except Vinnie, me, and our love.

Our lips meet in a kiss full of unspoken promises and shared fears. Waves of vulnerability crash over me as I realize the danger we're about to step into, but I can't ignore the flame burning brightly within me. For Vinnie, I'd brave any storm.

As we pull away from each other, he wipes away a stray tear from my cheek with his thumb, and I feel a sudden urge to memorize every line in his face—the rugged jawline, the stubble that always seems to be there, the weary lines etching the corners of his eyes. I study them all as if preparing myself for an unknown future where these memories might serve as my only solace.

"What are you doing?" he asks.

"Just memorizing," I whisper.

His eyes soften at my words. "Raven..."

The sound of my name rolling off his tongue tugs at something deep within me. I reach up to trace the contours of his face. As my fingers brush against his skin, Vinnie closes his eyes and leans into my touch.

"Raven," he murmurs again. His voice is filled with such tenderness that it sends shivers down my spine. "I wish we could have met under different circumstances."

I smile softly at him and place a hand on his chest. "I don't. Everything that's happened, everything we've both been through—it led us to each other. I wouldn't change that for the world."

He stares at me for what feels like an eternity. There's so much emotion in his gaze that it takes my breath away. Then, with a quiet "okay," he leans in to press his lips against mine once again.

The kiss is slow and passionate, filled with a kind of intensity that leaves me breathless. It's as though he's pouring every ounce of his emotions into the kiss, and I can't help but respond in kind.

He glides his hand under my tank top, his touch like fire. My nipples, already hard, ache for him.

I dig my fingers into his back and pull him even closer. He trails kisses down the side of my neck, making me shiver. His scent, a mix of musk and mint, drifts over me as his warm lips explore the curve of my shoulder.

"Vinnie," I whisper against his ear. My voice is shaky from the overwhelming sensations coursing through my body.

He pulls back slightly to look at me, his eyes dark with desire. He slides his fingers down the length of my spine, sending a ripple of pleasure through me. I reach up to tangle my hands in his wavy hair, pulling him closer for a kiss. He darts into my mouth, deepening the kiss, and I'm lost in the feel of him—the taste of him.

Suddenly he pulls back slightly and looks at me, his gaze intense and piercing. "Are you okay?" he asks, his voice barely above a whisper.

"I'm more than okay," I say, deliberately placing the fears in a cubicle in my head.

I want only now. This. With Vinnie.

Vinnie captures my lips once again, his hands exploring every inch of my body. His touch is electric, releasing currents of pleasure all through me.

He lifts me effortlessly, and I wrap my legs around his waist as we stumble toward the bed. He lays me down gently, never breaking the kiss. I love the feel of the weight of his body. It's comfort. It's passion. It's security.

He finds the hem of my tank top, and he pulls away from our kiss long enough to peel it off me. He slides his lips over my neck.

"God, Raven," he murmurs against my skin, his voice rough with need. "I want to make this night unforgettable for you."

"I trust you," I say through shallow breaths.

In a flash, Vinnie has shed his clothes and he stands before me naked and erect. So handsome and magnificent. I swallow as he moves my tank top over my head and then unbuttons my shorts. A moment later, I'm as naked as he is.

He caresses my thigh, pushing it gently to the side as he settles between my legs. He teases them with featherlight kisses on my inner thighs, drawing out lustful whimpers from me. A knowing smile tugs at the corners of his mouth as he looks at me.

"Vinnie," I gasp out when he brushes his hard cock against my pussy, barely touching it.

He explores further, each touch sending jolts of pleasure coursing through me. I dig my fingers into the sheets. As he continues his slow torture, I gasp out his name over and over again, each utterance more desperate than the last.

His eyes never leave mine as he works my pussy with his lips and tongue, driving me closer to the edge.

He's loving me. Truly loving me.

The world narrows down to him and me—his touch, my cries, our breaths mingling in this shared space. The tension coils inside me, winding tighter and tighter until I can hardly breathe.

"Vinnie," I plead.

With a final flick of his tongue coupled with a well-placed stroke of his fingers, I shatter into a million fragments. I tighten my grip on the sheets, arch my back, and cry out. The world spins around me, leaving me panting and trembling beneath him.

He continues to stroke me, guiding me through the aftershocks, his gaze never wavering from mine. I see a hint of pride in his eyes, satisfaction painted across his face as he watches me come undone because of him.

Slowly, my breathing returns to normal and I collapse on the soft sheets beneath me. Vinnie rises from between my legs, placing a tender kiss on my belly button before moving upward. He trails soft kisses along my rib cage, stopping to capture a hardened nipple between his lips.

God, the feeling... The overwhelming feeling...

He sucks on one nipple, plays with the other. I close my eyes, letting the rapture take me. So good, so good, so good...

He leaves my nipples, and then, the tear of a condom

packet and the familiar rustling as he rolls it on. He grips my thighs and pulls me closer to him.

"I want you, Vinnie. Please," I beg softly.

He groans as he thrusts into me.

Not gently.

And it's perfect.

I gasp at the sensation, stretch again to accommodate him. He gives me a second to adjust, and then he pulls out and thrusts back in, this time going deeper.

Emotion wells up inside me as he fills me completely. He leans down to capture my lips in a devouring kiss.

All the while he thrusts, thrusts, thrusts...

He breaks the kiss, sucking in a deep breath. "Raven," he whispers against my lips, his voice hoarse. "You feel so good."

I can only nod in agreement, incapable of forming a coherent response. I clutch at his back as he quickens the pace, each hard thrust sending waves of pleasure crashing over me.

The familiar coil tightens within me. His pace becomes more frenzied as he shifts and somehow goes even deeper.

I shatter then, releasing around him.

"Vinnie!" I cry out, my voice breaking as I dig my nails into his back.

He is relentless, pushing into me again and again and again and again. Faster, faster, and harder, harder...

Until—

"Raven," he gasps, his voice full of raw emotion.

He pulses into me, and I clamp my legs around his hips, taking all he has to give. I reach up to pull him down for a kiss, pouring all my feelings for him into it.

Vinnie breaks the kiss and lifts his head. His dark eyes

meet mine, and I see a raw intimacy in them that leaves me breathless all over again.

He pulls out slowly, and even in my satiated state, I can't help but whimper at the loss. He disappears for a moment, discarding the condom before returning to the bed with a damp cloth. His gentle touch as he cleans me is almost reverent, and it brings tears to my eyes.

But his body goes rigid.

Even after release, I can feel the tension rising within him.

Is it the drone? The Uber driver who forced me to call him?

Or is it something else?

32

VINNIE

When I first got to Europe, I was an ignorant young man of eighteen, but I knew one thing. No one could be trusted. Not even family. *Especially* family. I'd managed to take some money from my giant trust fund to live on, but I knew it wouldn't last forever, so I wasted no time getting new identification and then I did odd jobs throughout the EU as I traveled.

I wasn't completely honest with Savannah about why I went to the Buddhist temple.

It wasn't just to alleviate the guilt of leaving her and Mikey back in the States at the whim of the family. And it wasn't just to work through what my grandfather had done to me.

It was because I found myself involved in something far more sinister.

One fateful day, I ended up in a secluded alley in Prague, where a crooked wooden door creaked open to reveal an underground gambling den. There I met Misha—a man whose green eyes gleamed with dangerous amusement.

His real name was Mikhail, which threw me—the Slavic version of Michael. I thought of Mikey, who I'd left at home, and guilt overwhelmed me. When Misha offered me an opportunity to make a huge profit, part of me felt like I was talking to my brother, so I jumped in with both feet.

Misha was searching for a hidden treasure buried in the heart of Eastern Europe.

I was intrigued—and also desperate for some easy cash.

But it turned out not to be so easy. I dived into Misha's world, abandoning my odd jobs and my pursuit of quiet anonymity. He gave me a firearm but told me not to use it unless I had to defend myself.

A year passed. I lived in shadows and chased ghosts. Misha kept me busy while he sometimes disappeared for days at a time. His name notwithstanding, I didn't fully trust him, but I found myself enjoying the chase. Every time doubt crept in, Misha would return, always with a new clue, a new lead.

I got sucked in, and the whole thing became a game to me. Did I think we'd really find treasure? Maybe at the time I did. It gave me a creative outlet, something to do.

Until I realized it wasn't all that different from what I'd fled from at home.

I was becoming bound to a different kind of family. Not my mafia family, but an Eastern European underworld. Misha operated under different rules, but the principle was the same—secrets, power, betrayal.

I had to get out.

One cold night in Bucharest, I got my chance.

Misha told me he'd uncovered the final piece of the

puzzle, located within the grip of a rival gang. We'd need to be quick. We'd need to be strong.

"Are you afraid?" Misha asked me.

"No," I lied through gritted teeth.

"Good," he said. "Fear will only lead to your demise."

The gang had set up their base in an old chateau. The stone structure was imposing as hell and full of foreboding darkness.

As we moved through the corridors, our footsteps muffled by the worn-out rugs, my heart pounded. The echoes of raucous laughter and clinking glasses reached us, growing louder with each step we took. Misha led the way. He was in his element. Danger was his drug.

Until he turned on me.

To this day I don't know why. Maybe because I presented a challenge to him. Maybe he decided he wanted all the loot for himself. Or maybe he was just batshit crazy.

But that night, I did something I swore I'd never do.

I took a life.

It was self-defense, but I still had to move quickly and quietly to avoid being caught.

I learned to travel during the night. Change my identity and appearance when necessary.

And I was done with crime.

Done.

Until now, of course.

If everything went according to my plan, Puzo should be dead.

He was a piece of shit, and the world won't mourn him.

But doing my grandfather's bidding doesn't give me the revenge I crave.

The vengeful vice I've been carrying around with me since that fateful day in his office, where he violated me in the worst way while I refused to scream out in pain.

Because fuck him.

Fuck him and fuck the world that allowed him to exist. I left that life behind, buried it deep under layers of pseudonyms, fake passports, and never-ending roads. But the ghosts were always there, whispering in my ear, reminding me of all that had been taken from me.

I existed in the shadows, a phantom flitting through Europe. I eked out a living doing odd jobs, never staying in one place for too long. As long as I remained a ghost, I was safe.

But I'm back now.

And I'll have my revenge.

I regard Raven. She's sleeping soundly.

It kills me to leave her, but she has no place in the world I have to inhabit.

I can't shake the anger coursing through my veins. Every time I close my eyes, I see Misha's face, smirking, laughing as he turned on me.

He's not laughing now.

Grandfather thinks I'm weak. Too weak to take Puzo out with a gun he provided.

That doesn't make me weak. It makes me smart.

Grandfather doesn't know who he's dealing with. But he will soon enough.

Vengeance isn't just a fleeting thought for me. It's my driving force, my vice. It consumes me, and I welcome it.

Every step I take is fueled by the need to make Grandfather pay. I've lost so much because of him, and now it's my turn to take something. It won't bring back what I've lost, but it will satisfy this burning need inside me. He thinks he's untouchable, but his arrogance will be his downfall.

I'm a storm ready to unleash hell. He won't see it coming until it's too late. I'll be his reckoning. I'll be his nightmare. And when it's done, maybe then I'll find some peace.

Or maybe this vengeful vice will have consumed me completely, and there will be nothing left but the ashes of my own destruction.

But until then I will be relentless. Nothing will stand in my way. They will regret the day they crossed me. This isn't just a promise. It's my reality, my unyielding obsession.

I didn't mean to fall in love.

I didn't mean to drag an innocent woman into my underworld.

I press my lips to Raven's soft cheek.

Then I rise from the bed, dress quietly, and leave.

Never to see her again.

33

RAVEN

I'm sitting in the doctor's office. For weeks now I haven't felt like myself.

It started with headaches. The first one occurred after I had imbibed in a few extra drinks at dinner the night before, so I thought it was just a mild hangover. A couple of Advil and it went away. But then they kept coming back. More often than normal.

Then the fatigue. I used to be quite the night owl, often staying up until two or three in the morning. Now I'm lucky to make it past nine thirty. But I'm in my late twenties. Didn't seem too weird that I'd start prioritizing sleep more.

Then the pain in my joints, which I assumed was a result of me exercising too hard. Then the weight loss—did I change my diet without realizing it? Of course, I haven't had much of an appetite lately, so that could be it.

There's been a rational explanation behind every symptom I've experienced.

I made the mistake of mentioning it to my mom, and she of course went straight to Dr. Google. She found all sorts of debili-

tating diseases I could have, ranging from Lou Gehrig's disease to multiple sclerosis.

But she's a mother. Mothers are supposed to worry.

So I went to the doctor to get her off my back.

I described my symptoms to the doctor, and she didn't seem too troubled. They drew some of my blood for some tests a few days ago and then called me into the office to discuss the results.

My doctor—I think her name is Dr. Jenson—enters the room now. This is only the second time I've seen her. Before she drew my blood last week, I hadn't seen a doctor for anything other than my annual gyno exam since I was in college getting tested for STDs.

She walks into her office. "Thank you for coming in, Raven."

"Of course." I chuckle. "Anything to get my mother to stop worrying."

Dr. Jenson doesn't join me in laughing. She takes out a clipboard with several pieces of paper stacked on top of it. "We received the results of your bloodwork yesterday. I'm afraid it's a bit of bad news."

An invisible fist tightens around my heart. Bad news? I'm healthy as a horse. I never thought that this would be anything serious. Just a few weeks of feeling mildly shitty. Things like that tend to balance out.

Don't they?

I swallow. "What is it?"

Dr. Jenson takes a deep breath in. "You have cancer, Raven. Leukemia."

And my world goes black.

Cancer? That's a disease that other people get, not me. No one in my family has ever had cancer. I mean, I think I had a great-aunt who had skin cancer once, but she just had a mole removed and that was it.

Leukemia? That's serious. The kind of thing people die from.

"You're joking, right?" I stand up. "I feel fine, Dr. Jenson. I've just been a little out of sorts the past few weeks. Nothing serious."

"You are of course welcome to go see another physician for a second opinion," Dr. Jenson says. "But this kind of cancer can be aggressive. It would be in your best interest to start treatment right away."

Treatment? She means chemo. I bring my hand up to my thick tresses of dark hair. *I love my hair. I don't want it to go away. I don't...*

"Of course, if chemotherapy doesn't work, there are other options down the line that we can try. But they are invasive..."

The doctor might as well be speaking Swedish. Her words are no longer making sense. I sit there, nodding blankly.

After about three minutes of her speaking, I put a hand up. "Will I die?"

Dr. Jenson looks up at me, her gaze sympathetic but altogether far too businesslike. "With early treatment, the odds can be pretty good—"

"Give me a number, doctor. Please."

She clasps her hands together. "You have about a sixty-five percent chance of survival."

Sixty-five percent? That would be a D if I were in school getting a letter grade.

I guess it's better than fifty-fifty.

Phenomenal. I have a slightly better chance than a coin flip at living.

Dr. Jenson rattles on some more. I don't hear a word. Fifteen minutes later I leave the office with a handful of pamphlets and referrals.

I get to my home on my family's ranch. I place all the

pamphlets on my kitchen counter, strip off all my clothes, and lie down in my bed.

For an hour, I just feel empty. Shocked.

Then, ever so slowly, it hits me. Tiny bee stings, one at a time.

I have cancer.

I might die.

I'm going to lose my hair.

Oh, God, I have to tell my family.

And then the tears come. Just a few at first, but then a fountain erupts. I'm sobbing uncontrollably, clinging to my bedsheets for dear life.

They keep coming, and there's no turning them off. It is only in the wee hours of the morning that exhaustion takes over and I finally fall asleep.

The stream of sunlight through my window wakes me up early in the morning. I've only slept a few hours. For a second I wonder if it was all a bad dream.

And then I remember.

But I'm out of tears. Nothing can come. I'm numb.

Numb...except for a tiny flame that erupts deep in my core. A flame of resolve.

This flame will stay with me over the next several years of cancer treatment. Sometimes it grows, enveloping my entire body, and sometimes it is almost completely extinguished.

But it never leaves me.

Because I'm going to fight this horrible disease. I'm going to kill it.

Even if it kills me in the process.

~

The sun cascades through my window as I wake up. I rise, throw my legs over to the side of the bed, stretching my arms over my head.

Vinnie and I had sex last night.

Correction. We made *love.*

He said he loves me. And I told him I love him.

God, I don't know if I've ever been happier.

I look around. He's not here. Odd. I throw on a robe. Maybe he's an early riser, got up to make a pot of coffee.

I saunter into the kitchen, yawning. "Vinnie?"

But he's not here.

Maybe he had an early meeting with that grandfather of his. Certainly he'd have left me a note, though, right?

I'll check my phone. Maybe he left me a text.

I turn on the screen. No texts at all since last night.

Including from Brick. I check to make sure the text I sent him canceling our date went through. It did.

He was probably pissed at me for flaking at the last minute. I can't blame him. I sigh. I guess I'll have to find another lawyer to help me out with the nonprofit.

But Vinnie didn't text me, which is weird.

I put the phone down. I'm about to start a pot of coffee when it rings.

It's my mom. Damn it. I didn't text her last night to let her know I'd be spending the night at my place. She'll be beside herself with worry.

"Hello?"

"Raven, thank God."

Mom's voice is high-pitched and energetic. I can hear a lot of hustle and bustle in the background. The house seems very active for early in the morning.

"Yeah, I'm sorry I forgot to call you last night."

"Are you at your place?"

"I am."

"Thank God." Mom's voice is still pretty frantic.

My heart begins to race, but I'm not sure why. All I know is something isn't right here.

"Is anything the matter?" I gasp. "Is something wrong with Dad?"

"No, sweetheart. Your father and I are fine. But we..." She lets out a choking sob.

"Mom, what's wrong?"

But she can't seem to get herself together. Something is very wrong here.

"Can you put Dad on?"

Mom blubbers out some words I can't make out, but then I hear my dad's voice on the receiver.

"Raven. Didn't you have a date with that lawyer last night?"

"I did." The guilt hits me again. "But I... I wasn't feeling too great, so I canceled it."

Dad's tone is artificially even. "Did you cancel it at the very last minute?"

"I did."

"I see." Dad pauses. "Your mother and I went to a movie last night. We got back late and went straight to bed. This morning, she got up to check on you, and..."

"What, Dad? I wasn't there? I'm sorry, I should have called to—"

"No, it's not that." Dad clears his throat. "She found... someone else in your bed."

My blood runs cold. "*What?*"

"Yes." Dad pauses. "It was...a body."

My heart is pounding out of my chest. "A body? Like...a *dead* body?"

"Yes." Dad's voice is shaking through the phone. "The lawyer. Mr. Latham. His throat slit wide open."

Oh my God, oh my *God...*

"There was a note on your nightstand next to him. Handwriting I don't recognize."

A note? Oh God, did he kill himself? He seemed pretty level-headed. Surely a broken date wouldn't be something that would drive him to...

There's no way.

I draw in a shaky breath. "What did it say?" I whisper.

I can hear Dad shudder from the other end of the line before he finally speaks again.

"*Your move, Cobra.*"

EXCERPT FROM THE PERILS OF PATRICIA

CHAPTER ONE

Lady Patricia Price-Adams, known to most of her acquaintances simply as Tricia, perched on the edge of her grand four-poster bed, a stolen underground magazine between her fingers. The forbidden inked words seemed to dance before her eyes, each salacious detail more shocking than the last. An unwed lady of the peerage with such boundless sensual experience? Who would continue her secret trysts once she was married? Tricia couldn't wait to read more.

Lady Sarah Keating, Tricia's dearest friend and confidant, had discovered this hidden gem within the clandestine folds of her maid's linens. And now, here it was, igniting a spark of wild curiosity in Tricia's soul.

Tricia and Sarah were both on the cusp of their societal debuts, and Sarah had insisted that a glimpse into the unspoken escapades of ladies and gentlemen in the bedchamber would be enlightening. But the stories within *The Ruby* blurred the lines of propriety so thoroughly that

Tricia doubted the honorifics of *gentleman* or *lady* could be reasonably applied to their characters.

The bedchamber around her whispered tales of luxury she'd only known for the past three years. She was still enthralled by all of it. Gilded frames embraced paintings of pastoral scenes and ancestors with stern gazes who would surely have disapproved of her reading material. The walls were adorned with richly patterned wallpaper the color of deep burgundy with swirls of gold that caught the light from the flickering candles in sconces. It created an atmosphere both warm and suffocating, much like the society outside her door.

Nearby, a plush chaise longue invited repose, its velvet upholstery a shade of emerald-green that complemented the room's opulence. Delicate lace draperies billowed gently at the windows, parting just enough to permit slivers of the waning afternoon sun. It bathed the chamber in a soft glow that highlighted the vanity opposite the bed.

Tricia scanned the pages eagerly, drinking in every lurid detail as she partook in the erotic fiction.

I'd love to taste your sweet nectar, Lady Portia.

Tell me of a young maiden being courted by two suitors, one dark, one blond. Tell me what they both wish to do to her in private.

What might it be like to feel such unrestrained passion, to step outside the confines of her gilded cage? Her fingertips absently drifted to the pearls that adorned her throat, a gift from her grandfather, the Marquess of Denbigh.

Oh!

The marquess would be shocked at what she was reading,

even though he was only her grandfather because of an illicit dalliance he had once shared with a housemaid.

The clock chimed three times in the distance, its dulcet tones echoing through the silence. She wanted to continue her reading, but when someone knocked at her door, she startled, hastily folding the paper and stowing it beneath a few plush pillows.

She rose from her bed, hoping she looked nonchalant, though her cheeks were burning. As she opened the heavy oak door, it creaked, revealing her maid, Trudy, whose presence was as comforting as the warm hearth on a winter's day.

"Pardon me, my lady," Trudy said, a tremor of urgency in her voice. "Your presence is requested in the parlor."

"For what purpose?"

"I cannot say, my lady. The countess... She's in distress." Trudy's eyes mirrored her concern.

Tricia gasped, and she clasped her hand to her lips to muffle the sound. The countess was Tricia's sister-in-law, Rose, who was married to her brother, Cameron, heir to the Marquess of Denbigh. Rose was a gentle and contented soul, so her tears were no trivial matter.

Urgency lent speed to Tricia's steps as she hastened to the parlor, nearly colliding with her younger sister, Lady Katrina Price-Adams, a sprite of ten with light-brown hair and eyes.

"Tricia," Katrina said, "what is going on?"

Tricia mustered a smile, though it felt as brittle as thin ice. "We shall find out together, Kitty Kat." She placed her hand gently on her sister's shoulder.

They descended the winding staircase, passing servants whose whispers darted about like startled sparrows, their routines disrupted as they prematurely prepared tea.

"It's too early for tea," Katrina murmured, her young brow creased.

"Yes, love," Tricia replied, her own nerves taut as violin strings.

Hand in hand, the sisters stepped into the parlor, a room now heavy with a sorrow that clung to the opulent draperies and the plush midnight-blue brocade of the davenport. There, they found their mother, Lady Clementine Price-Adams, a pillar of strength even as her eyes betrayed her concern.

But it was Rose who drew Tricia's gaze. Still blond and beautiful but weeping softly, she was cradled in Cameron's protective embrace.

"Mummy"—Tricia's voice barely breached the hushed reverence of the room—"what has happened?"

Lady Clementine met her daughter's gaze. "It's terrible news, my dears. The father of our beloved Rose has passed on."

The words fell like heavy stones into the stillness, and a new silence blanketed the parlor.

Tricia dropped her jaw. "Oh my!"

"Still such a young man, too." Her mother dabbed at her eyes with a handkerchief. "I'm dreadfully sorry for the countess. I suppose she's the dowager countess now. I know only too well what it is like to lose one's beloved husband."

Indeed, Tricia's own father had passed away when she was quite young. Kat hardly remembered him at all.

Tricia walked toward her sister-in-law. "Rose, I'm so sorry."

Rose sniffled into her handkerchief. "It was just so sudden. The physicians don't seem to know anything that I can tell. Of course, I must leave for Hampshire in the morning."

"We all will, darling," Cameron said.

"Of course," Lady Clementine agreed.

Tricia nodded, though she worried a bit about what it would mean for coming-out season.

She was only eighteen years old. If she couldn't come out this season, she would still be quite young for the next. She had argued and argued with Cameron about coming out. Rose hadn't come out until she was twenty, and she'd hardly had a season at all because, although she was courted by a young lord, her sister, Lily, met and fell in love with the Duke of Lybrook and married quickly, which led to Rose meeting Tricia's brother, who composed the waltz for Lily and the duke's wedding.

Tricia and her brother and sister were not highborn. They found out only after Cameron asked for Rose's hand that they were the grandchildren of the Marquess of Denbigh. His elderly mother, the dowager marchioness, saw Cameron at a theater production for which he had composed the music. He bore a striking resemblance to her son, and Tricia soon found that her father, Colton Price, was the son of a housemaid and fathered by the Marquess of Denbigh.

Overnight, they became members of the ton.

"I shall take care of everything, my sweet." Cameron kissed Rose's tear-stained cheek. "I suppose this means your brother is now the earl."

Her brother…

Viscount Thomas Jameson had ensnared Tricia's heart three years past. The viscount, a striking figure with sable hair and a perpetually shadowed jaw who carried his muscled physique with an easy grace, was still unmarried at one-and-thirty.

To him, Tricia was but a shadow, yet she was resolute to cast a light that would garner his notice in the coming season.

Viscount Jameson.

But no longer Viscount Jameson. He was now Thomas Jameson, the Earl of Ashford.

And...

He would be looking for a wife.

A NOTE FROM HELEN

Dear Reader,

Thank you for reading *Vengeful Vice*. If you want to find out about my current backlist and future releases, please visit my website, like my Facebook page, and join my mailing list. If you're a fan, please join my Facebook street team (Hardt & Soul) to help spread the word about my books. I regularly do awesome giveaways for my street team members.

If you enjoyed the story, please take the time to leave a review. I welcome all feedback.

I wish you all the best!

Helen

Sign up for my newsletter here:

http://www.helenhardt.com/signup

ALSO BY HELEN HARDT

My Heart Still Beats

Bellamy Brothers

Savage Sin

Sweet Sin

Seductive Sin

Vengeful Vice

Volatile Vice

Victorious Vice

Follow Me Series

Follow Me Darkly

Follow Me Under

Follow Me Always

Darkly

Under

Always

Black Rose Series

Blush

Bloom

Blossom

Wolfes of Manhattan

Rebel

Recluse

Runaway

Rake

Reckoning

Escape

Moonstone

Raven

Garnet

Buck

Opal

Phoenix

Amethyst

Sex and the Season

Lily and the Duke

Rose in Bloom

Lady Alexandra's Lover

Sophie's Voice

The Perils of Patricia

Steel Brothers Saga

Craving

Obsession

Possession

Melt

Burn

Surrender

Shattered

Twisted

Unraveled

Breathless

Ravenous

Insatiable

Fate

Legacy

Descent

Awakened

Cherished

Freed

Spark

Flame

Blaze

Smolder

Flare

Scorch

Chance

Fortune

Destiny

Melody

Harmony

Encore

Blood Bond Saga

Unchained

Unhinged

Undaunted

Unmasked

Undefeated

Temptation Saga

Tempting Dusty

Teasing Annie

Taking Catie

Taming Angelina

Treasuring Amber

Trusting Sydney

Tantalizing Maria

The Billion Heirs (with Vanessa Vale)

Scarred

Flawed

Broken

Non-Fiction

got style?

Cooking with Hardt & Soul

ACKNOWLEDGMENTS

Thank you so much to my editor (and son!) Eric J. McConnell; my beta readers, Corinne Akers, Serena Drummond, Karen Aguilera, and Linda Dunn; my cover artist, Amanda Shepard of Shepard Originals; and my audiobook narrators, Eric J. McConnell and Kaileigh Riess. You all helped *Vengeful Vice* shine!

ABOUT THE AUTHOR

#1 *New York Times*, #1 *USA Today*, and #1 *Wall Street Journal* bestselling author Helen Hardt's passion for the written word began with the books her mother read to her at bedtime. She wrote her first story at age six and hasn't stopped since. In addition to being an award-winning author of romantic fiction, she's a mother, an attorney, a black belt in Taekwondo, a grammar geek, an appreciator of fine red wine, and a lover of Ben and Jerry's ice cream. She writes from her home in Colorado, where she lives with her family. Helen loves to hear from readers.

Please sign up for her newsletter here:

http://www.helenhardt.com/signup

Visit her here:

http://www.helenhardt.com

Printed in Great Britain
by Amazon

53723207R00169